P9-APH-870

# This Nicole Hart was *hot!*

But not in any obvious way, Anthony thought. No black leather miniskirt, no three-inch spike heels. Hers was a quiet, but still incredibly sexy, kind of hot.

Everything about her said "Touch me." And he was afraid the only way he could keep himself from doing just that was to sit on his hands. This woman was out to make him lose control on camera—and she had the equipment to do it.

And she knew it. Oh, yes, she knew it....

It had only been a minute or two since she'd joined him on the set, but it already seemed like hours. Taking a deep breath, he looked up into her eyes. They telegraphed her intention of enjoying every excruciatingly slow moment of the half hour of torture she clearly had planned for him.

Well, at least he was no longer *bored....*

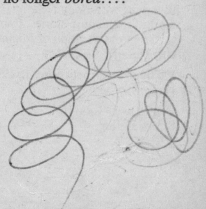

Dear Reader,

Welcome again to another exciting lineup from Temptation. The Lovers & Legends miniseries continues—each month a fairy tale retold sizzling Temptation-style!

This month, our Lovers & Legends title, *Naughty Talk* by Tiffany White, has—as you would expect from Tiffany—a lot of naughty talk! Based on the legend of Sir Gawain, who took as his quest the answer to the eternal question What Do Women Want?, Tiffany gives this legend her own naughty but amusing spin. In December, Kristine Rolofson concludes this special miniseries with *I'll Be Seeing You,* a wonderfully romantic, five-hankie version of Dickens's *A Christmas Carol.*

Just around the corner is 1994 and more excitement from Temptation. *Earth, wind, fire, water... the four elements—but nothing is more elemental than passion.* Join us for Passion's Quest, one book a month January to April will be an adventure story revolving around one of the elements beginning with *Body Heat* by Elise Title. Four fantastic adventure stories, four fantastic love stories in the tradition of *Romancing the Stone* and *The African Queen.*

We'll have other surprises in 1994, as well! Happy reading.

Birgit Davis-Todd
Senior Editor

# Naughty Talk

## Tiffany White

# Harlequin Books

TORONTO • NEW YORK • LONDON
AMSTERDAM • PARIS • SYDNEY • HAMBURG
STOCKHOLM • ATHENS • TOKYO • MILAN
MADRID • WARSAW • BUDAPEST • AUCKLAND

If you purchased this book without a cover you should be aware that this book is stolen property. It was reported as "unsold and destroyed" to the publisher, and neither the author nor the publisher has received any payment for this "stripped book."

For my friend Kathy Stohldrier who has expert taste and my friend Anthony Berin whose great smile should get him the job with the best tools when he grows up

ISBN 0-373-25565-9

NAUGHTY TALK

Copyright © 1993 by Anna Eberhardt.

All rights reserved. Except for use in any review, the reproduction or utilization of this work in whole or in part in any form by any electronic, mechanical or other means, now known or hereafter invented, including xerography, photocopying and recording, or in any information storage or retrieval system, is forbidden without the written permission of the publisher, Harlequin Enterprises Limited, 225 Duncan Mill Road, Don Mills, Ontario, Canada M3B 3K9.

All characters in this book have no existence outside the imagination of the author and have no relation whatsoever to anyone bearing the same name or names. They are not even distantly inspired by any individual known or unknown to the author, and all incidents are pure invention.

This edition published by arrangement with Harlequin Enterprises B. V.

® and TM are trademarks of the publisher. Trademarks indicated with ® are registered in the United States Patent and Trademark Office, the Canadian Trade Marks Office and in other countries.

Printed in U.S.A.

# 1

*Los Angeles Times*

Entertainment News:

ITEM ... "The Anthony Gawain Show" will feature a running theme during sweeps week. The bad boy of talk TV will be asking, *What do women want?* While this columnist thinks Gawain the Swain could do this show solo, what with his legendary prowess with women, we hear thus far that a top fashion model, a feminist writer and a popular lovelorn adviser have been scheduled.

"GAWAIN THE PAIN is more like it," Nicole Hart muttered, scanning the newspaper column.

"Still in a funk about being dumped from Anthony's show, are we?" Rafael Contreras asked, as he strolled into the small employees' lounge of Le Bistro in time to hear her complaint. The two of them waited tables at the restaurant while pursuing other careers;

Nicole was writing screenplays and Rafael studied costume design at UCLA.

Le Bistro's atmosphere was typical of L.A.—casual and friendly. Beneath huge bleached-canvas umbrellas, the bamboo tables were set informally with tiny bouquets of fresh flowers and jars of toasted breadsticks. Trendy foods like goat cheese, polenta and jalapeños were listed on the menu. It was, however, the chef's airy dessert confections that kept the customers lingering while classical music tinkled in the background.

Making himself at home, Rafe sat down beside Nicole and took a sip of her lemonade.

"That's bumped, not dumped," she retorted, taking back her drink.

Rafe shrugged a noncommittal shoulder, then reached to lift the Friday edition of the L.A. *Times* from her hands. His gaze was snagged by the Entertainment News item she'd been reading. "Hmm... Two vacancies for Gawain's show..." He shot her a considering look. "You know, it's your image that's the problem. Let's jazz up the way you dress. I bet if we did, we could get you on the show."

"There is nothing wrong with the way I dress."

Rafe gave her a bemused look.

"Well, there isn't," Nicole insisted, pushing her chin-length brown hair behind her ear. "Your problem is that you see life as one big movie, and you're the costume designer."

"Maybe," he agreed. "But you have to admit I know about clothes."

"Okay, what's wrong with the way I dress?" she asked, humoring him.

"Nothing, if you want to look like someone's invisible kid sister. Ever since you ran into the sleaze factor in Hollywood you've been dressing in oversize shirts and baggy jeans. Grunge is hardly the look to impress a cool dude like Anthony Gawain."

Nicole closed her eyes. He was right. She had definitely run into the sleaze factor when she'd been slogging her screenplays around town. But she didn't like the note of hero worship in Rafe's voice when he spoke Anthony's name. "Rafe, surely you can find a better role model than Anthony Gawain."

"You've got to be kidding...." His long fingers tapped the newspaper. "It says right here in Entertainment News that he gets all the babes."

"Well, I have no interest in being a *babe*. And I have even less interest in pleasing a man like Anthony Gawain."

Rafe laid down the newspaper he'd been scanning. "I think I'll come back later to ask you to work for me tomorrow night—sometime when you're in a kinder, gentler mood."

"What makes you think I don't have a date? I could have plans, you know," she said, baiting him.

"Do you?"

"No."

Unfortunately, Rafe knew her all too well; knew she spent all her energy on her fledgling career as a screenwriter. Their close relationship was built on a shared goal of success in the movies—plus their caring natures, which they disguised with caustic banter. Either would rather die than admit they were sentimental slobs; L.A. wasn't exactly a sentimental town.

"Okay, if you need to study, I'll work for you," she agreed, though it had never really been in question.

"Thanks," he said, not making eye contact.

Noticing his expression, she made a grab for the newspaper. "Wait a minute! The Lakers are playing, aren't they?"

Rafe's smile was sheepish.

"Okay, but you owe me one," she said on a laugh.

Picking up his order pad, Rafe stood and headed for the door of the employees' lounge. Stopping halfway there, he turned. "So if you aren't hot for Gawain's bod, like every other female in L.A., then why did you want to be on his show?"

Nicole didn't recall having said she wasn't hot for Gawain's bod. She'd moved to L.A. from the Midwest, not from another planet. But she saw no reason to point out to Rafe how attractive she found the talk-show host.

No, the package was fine. Very fine.

It was his image she had a problem with. Gawain the Swain. Now, really...

"Since the topic of Gawain's show that day was how movies are made, my having worked as an extra gave me an entrée. I wanted to meet the director who was on that show. I need to start networking in the industry if I'm ever going to get my script read. Or at least, until I get an agent.

"Unfortunately, Gawain's producer uses the show to troll for 'babes.' He bumped me from the show in favor of a starlet he was cuddling with backstage."

"At least the producer has relationships...."

"Rafe..."

"Well, it's true, Nicole. The few times you've dated, they've been men who weren't up to your speed," he said, warming to his favorite topic—her love life, or the lack thereof. Of course, compared to Rafe, a rabbit lived a cloistered life-style.

"Go!" She shooed him away.

Alone in the employees' lounge, she looked out the window at the lingering showers brought by a cold front that had now moved east. Sighing, she stared sightlessly at the raindrops chasing each other down the windowpane.

Much as she hated to admit it, Rafe was right.

Relationships with men were something she shied away from. Of course, Rafe didn't count—he was the brother she'd never had.

The only kind of relationship she wanted with a man was an ideal, romantic one; one where love wasn't transitory. But if someone as beautiful as her mother, who played the decorative, submissive role so well, couldn't hold a man, what were the chances that she could? After all, her mother had married three handsome, charismatic men; men who'd had nothing in common but their looks—and their leaving.

Having grown up without a stable male influence, she was at a distinct disadvantage when it came to understanding or trusting men—though she understood men like Gawain and the producer of his show well enough. She was still steamed about that experience.

She had been wronged.

And someone ought to pay. Such sexist behavior shouldn't go unchallenged. She'd been a coward to say nothing at the time. Celebrities like Anthony Gawain, celebrities who were exactly the wrong kind of role model, ought to at least be called on it.

But she didn't want to be strident or militant about it. No one listened to fanatics. What she needed was a way to make her point without committing professional suicide.

Recalling Rafe's offer to jazz up her image to get her on the talk show made her smile. It was an offer he was forever making. If she let him, he'd turn her into his very own brown-haired, brown-eyed Barbie doll, trying out all his wild ideas on her. But then again maybe she ought to take him up it. After all, he owed her. . . .

Her smile grew into a wide grin. A wicked one.

Her idea was pure deceit. Would she really dare it? No, she couldn't—could she?

But the idea refused to go away. It was oh-so-tempting. What if she got herself on his What Do Women Want? show—as the hottest, sexiest sex therapist ever.

She'd minored in drama in college—and she *was* a screenwriter, after all—so with Rafe's help, she should be able to pull off the scam.

She laughed out loud.

She would give Anthony Gawain a sex therapist who'd peel the paint right off the studio walls. And once she was on-camera, she'd turn up the heat until he burned.

MARK BATES WATCHED Anthony Gawain tilt back the scarred wooden restaurant chair, balancing it precariously on two legs while he scanned the morning mail and yesterday's newspaper.

Mark envied the star of the talk show he produced.

Anthony had the good looks of a model and wore his clothing like one; clothing he bought anywhere from Armani to the Gap. The long, sleek black hair that fell to Anthony's shoulders was the first thing one noticed about him. Especially if, like Mark, you were starting to lose your hair. Anthony's luxuriant mane telegraphed his attitude—no one told him what to do or what to think.

There could be no doubt he was a rebel. The unusual thing about him, though, was that he was a rebel from the *right* side of the tracks. His family were *the* Gawains of a political dynasty; grandfather, father, uncles, cousins and younger brother.

Mark knew Anthony wasn't crazy about having him produce his talk show. A nephew of one of the network's bigwigs, Mark had been foisted upon Anthony as part of the deal. They would never be friends—Anthony was too much of a loner to have an entourage—but the two of them managed a working relationship.

They met weekly for breakfast at Patrick's Roadhouse to map out upcoming shows.

Landing the chair back on all fours to the black-and-white tile floor, Anthony folded the newspaper and handed it to Mark.

"See about booking this guy on the show," he instructed, pointing out an article about an eighty-year-old gambler who'd outlived all his enemies.

"Done," Mark agreed as a cute young waitress brought them their Spanish omelets. She didn't giggle or ask for Anthony's autograph. Patrick's Roadhouse was a celebrity hangout, and at any given time there were enough actors on hand to cast a movie or two.

"Did you see we got a mention on our sweeps-week show in the Entertainment News column?" Mark asked, lifting a forkful of warm, oniony omelet to his lips. The sharp bite of peppery salsa lingered on his tongue after he swallowed.

"Yeah, I saw it. I do wish that woman would concentrate more on the content of my shows and less on her invention of my reputation as a ladies' man."

"So we'll tell her to lay off," Mark said, not understanding his boss's beef at all. He would have loved to have press like that himself.

Anthony shrugged the subject off.

"Coming from a political family like mine, you learn early on that the press prints more fiction than fact," he observed. "Sometimes it's the subject who misleads the press, and sometimes it's the press who mislead the public. No matter. Everyone has an agenda, and most of the time it's a hidden one. Hidden agendas fascinate me. Or, more precisely, the reasons behind them."

"Why?"

"Why? Well, for instance, aren't you curious about why women lie to you?"

"Not particularly. Unlike you, I'm not all that interested in talk," Mark said, winking broadly.

"Well, I for one would like to find a woman honest enough to say what she really wants." Anthony stopped and frowned. "Who've we got as possible guests for the last two shows of our sweeps-week series?"

Mark pulled out his notes. "A wife and mother, a career military officer, a sex therapist and an actress."

"The wife and mother," Anthony said right off. He took his time considering the other options, then declared, "And the sex therapist. Let's just see what sort of hidden agenda a sex therapist has."

NICOLE SLUMPED DOWN in the padded wicker rocker and allowed the cozy warmth of the rough-shingled cottage to soothe her. She was house-sitting for an actress who was making a movie-of-the-week in Rome.

"Wow! This place is great!" Rafe said, bringing in the packages from the car. He dropped the shopping bags on the hardwood floor, then flopped down on the sofa.

"You should see the place I'm house-sitting," he said, making a face. "It's all mirrors and shiny surfaces."

"You know you love it," Nicole teased, taking in Rafe's perfect profile. "I still can't believe you don't want to be an actor, with your good looks." He was the first and best friend she'd made since moving to L.A. six months ago and starting work at Le Bistro. Rafe was the one who'd gotten her into the house-sitting network used by Hollywood hopefuls.

"Do you really think I can pull this off?" Nicole asked. She was beginning to have second thoughts. "Maybe this isn't such a good idea. No one is going to believe I'm a sex therapist."

"'The Anthony Gawain Show' believed it. I got you booked, didn't I?" Rafe reminded.

"You haven't said exactly how you did that...."

"And I don't intend to. It's enough that I made good use of the glamour shot I forced you to have done and the bio I had a friend write. You aren't the only one who can pull off a scam, you know."

"I just wish I wasn't so nervous," Nicole said, slipping off her shoes. Why had she thought this was such a good idea? What would pulling off this scam gain her besides a bit of revenge?

Fun. She needed an antidote to the continual rejection that most newcomers encountered in the movie business.

"You'll do fine," Rafe assured her. "Have you told your family what you're up to?"

Oh, blast! She hadn't thought about anyone she knew watching the show. "Are you kidding? My two married sisters worry about me as it is. And Mother is who knows where, traveling with a rodeo star who's half her age. I think the last postcard I got from her said she was somewhere in Montana."

"You take after your mother, you know," Rafe said, not for the first time. He loved the idea of her mother's madcap life.

"Hush your mouth, Rafe."

"I can't believe how casual your family ties are. If my brother, sister and I didn't show up every week for Sunday dinner, we'd be disowned."

Rafe's family sounded both confining and wonderful, to Nicole. She couldn't resist teasing him. "Gee, all you need in your family for a Kodak moment is grandbabies."

"Hush your mouth," Rafe parroted. "I am way too young to get married."

"I don't think age has anything to do with it. From the research I did for Gawain's show, I'd say a lasting marriage in the nineties is an even longer shot than my screenplay getting into production. As I see it, marriage is like development hell."

"What?"

"You know, like when a screenplay goes into development. In theory, it's a good idea, but in reality...there're just too many reasons why it won't work out."

"How is your screenplay coming, by the way?"

"Don't ask." At the moment, the only thing she liked about it was the title, "Cat and Spouse." It was a romantic comedy and she was having trouble with the ending. In the six months she'd been in L.A., she'd found out just how hard it was to sell a screenplay. This was her third script, and she just knew she was going to sell it—despite the odds; despite the sleazy con artists and real movie producers she'd connected with so far. She really should get an agent.

"Oh, well, maybe going on the show will inspire you," Rafe said. "What are you planning to talk about?"

"I thought I'd bring up how women's needs have changed in the nineties. Not every woman is waiting for her prince to come. Even Princess Di has found out that isn't what it's cracked up to be. For many women, revolving their life around a man has lost its appeal."

"Nicole?"

"What?"

"Remind me not to let my dates within a hundred yards of you. That is, unless you're planning on treating us to dinner with the loot you're getting from your fee for guesting on Gawain's show."

"Good idea, but I'm not keeping the fee."

"What?"

"I'm donating it to a charity—Big Sisters, maybe. That gets me off the hook for what I'm doing."

"With your conscience, maybe. But you'd better be careful Gawain doesn't find you out. I don't think you'd get off the hook too easily with him."

"I'm not worried about him," Nicole said, hoping she sounded more confident than she felt. "I'm a writer. I can think fast."

"You've got a point," Rafe agreed. He began removing the clothes he'd chosen for her to wear on the talk show from the shopping bag. "I think you're going to pull off a great scam. There's just one thing I regret," he said, pulling out a pair of sexy, strappy sandals.

"What's that?" Nicole asked.

Rafe slipped the sandal on her bare foot. "That I'm not going to get a wardrobe credit for the show."

ANTHONY GAWAIN WAS bored.

The overnight ratings for the first four shows of his sweeps-week series had been respectable, but he'd found the answers his guests had given him more than a little predictable.

The model had wanted a man to love her for who-ever she was beneath the one-hour makeup job, and the feminist, of course, had wanted to be treated equally. The lovelorn columnist was of the opinion that the majority of women wanted to be treated in the traditional way, while the housewife and mother just wanted someone who would *help*.

None of the women had shown much evidence of a sense of humor.

Was that what the war between the sexes had set-tled into? A cold war? An uneasy truce in which both sides tolerated each other through necessity?

Maybe he hadn't asked the right questions.

Maybe his guests were boring.

Or maybe *he* was boring.

He knew he took women for granted, much as the culture did. But at least he recognized it—recognized that his relationships were pretty shallow. Maybe he was going through some sort of period of personal growth. All he knew was that, although he knew the truth about a lot of things, he pretty much kept blinders on when it came to looking at himself.

What he wanted was some sort of exciting dialogue with a woman.

He didn't hold out much hope that the guest for today's show would be that woman.

The sex therapist Mark had booked was late.

As he clipped the microphone to his tie, a wild print of scattered pink Cadillac cars, he wondered if his audience had picked up on his lack of interest. He was going to have to snap out of it before his show suffered.

His television success had been very satisfying. And the fact that his success annoyed the hell out of his family was even more satisfying—hard work—nothing more, nothing less—had put him where he was. Lately, however, he'd begun to find his obsession tiring. Maybe he was taking life too seriously, as Mark often told him. Or maybe it wasn't life, but himself he was taking too seriously.

One thing he knew for certain—he damn well wasn't having half the fun the Entertainment News columnist seemed to think he was.

"Okay, look alive, Gawain. We're on in five... four... three...."

Gawain smiled into the camera. That was something that got harder to do with each show.

"Let's welcome sex therapist Nicole Hart," he said.

He turned to look hopefully for her entrance. His jaw dropped as he watched her approach.

"I'm pleased to be invited to be on your show, Mr. Gawain," she said, taking the seat across from him.

"Anthony. Call me Anthony." Suddenly he was sweating. It had nothing to do with the bright stage lights. He was used to them.

From the corner of his eye he saw the wide smile of the cameraman.

Nicole Hart was *hot!*

But not in any obvious way. There was no black leather miniskirt, no three-inch spike heels. Hers was a quiet, but still incredibly sexy kind of hot.

In her eyes was a molten look of challenge, their chocolate color rich with dark secrets. Everything about her said, "Touch me." He was very much afraid the only way to keep himself from doing just that was to sit on his hands. This was a woman out to make him lose control on-camera—and she had the equipment to do it with ease.

But why?

And how was he going to hold an intelligent conversation with her, when all the while her pouting lips slicked with mat berry-stain beckoned and the studiously casual muss of her shiny brown hair cried out to be touched?

And her outfit—a gray washed-silk jacket and matching pants . . . The fabric clung provocatively to every curve of her body as she moved, teasing him, daring him to touch and feel the bare skin beneath.

Her collarless jacket plunged all the way to the one-button closure at her waist. And under the jacket was nothing—nothing but temptation.

Nothing but bare sun-kissed skin to drive him crazy. And she knew it.

While he tried to remember what it was he'd been about to ask her, she crossed her legs and offered up the hint of a pleased smile.

Her feet were clad in flat, strappy sandals of grayish metallic leather. Instantly he felt himself developing a foot fetish. And for a brief, insane moment, he wondered if it might not be worth it to end his career by sucking her toes on-camera.

It had only been a minute or two since she'd joined him, but it had seemed like hours. Taking a deep breath, he gained control at last. He looked back up into her eyes. They telegraphed her intention of enjoying every excruciatingly slow moment of the half hour of torture she clearly had planned.

Well, at least he was no longer bored. . . .

# 2

ANTHONY GAWAIN HAD balls—she'd give him that.

The set of his talk show consisted of two yellow-and-rose chintz love seats set at right angles to some scarred pieces of pine furniture. The furniture wasn't television-new, but worn and lived-in. It took a man unafraid of his feminine side to pull this look off.

Rather sardonically, Nicole considered two things: One was that the setting wasn't intimidating. It seemed designed to lull guests into relaxing enough to unwittingly say more than they might if on guard. The second was the fact that Anthony Gawain no doubt knew how very attractively masculine the somewhat feminine setting made him appear.

She watched him shrug out of the two-thousand-dollar Armani jacket he'd worn with jeans, and wondered just what he was up to. She knew she'd unnerved him—as planned—and she was waiting for his counterpunch.

Waiting and ready.

"Well, shall we get down to business, then?" he said, unbuttoning the cuffs of his shirt after casually tossing off his expensive jacket.

Ah, here was the counterpunch, she thought as he began rolling the sleeves of his shirt to his elbows, revealing strong, sinewy forearms dusted with hair the same sleek dark texture as the long hair he'd pulled back in a ponytail. He looked more the rock impresario or the drug dealer than the son of one of the most powerful political dynasties in America.

"I'm ready whenever you're comfortable," Nicole replied. The crowd tittered in response to the implicit suggestion that he was more than a little uncomfortable in her presence.

He considered her, one dark eyebrow raised. He started to say something, then thought better of it, settling back into the cushy sofa instead. She took note when he pulled his ankle across his knee, revealing protective body language, chapter and verse.

Nicole smiled, unable to stop herself. She reprimanded herself for taking pleasure in her charade, told herself she shouldn't be enjoying someone else's discomfort so. But it didn't do any good. Today she was playing hookey from being trustworthy. Today she was a woman scorned. Today Anthony Gawain was going to pay. And she was going to enjoy it.

He cleared his throat. "So, Miss Hart, what *do* women want?"

"What do you think they want?" she countered, catching him off guard.

"Ah...ah..." He turned his hands palms up in a gesture of uncertainty. It was clearly a question he hadn't given much prior thought to. Flailing about, he finally came up with, "Oh, I don't know. I suppose Kevin Costner would be the man of the hour."

"Kevin Costner?"

Anthony nodded.

Chewing her berry-stained lips, she toyed with the silver disk at her earlobe and let him twist in the wind. "I find it rather interesting and markedly conceited that you think a *man* is what a woman wants—and a celebrity at that. Tell me, Anthony, does Kim Basinger rank number one on your list of what you want?"

His shrug was careless, but his green eyes narrowed at her game. "Kim Basinger is a fine-looking woman. A man would have to be dead not to appreciate her," he replied, cleverly evasive. "You mean to tell me you don't want Kevin Costner, Miss Hart?"

"Call me Nikki," she said playfully. "And my answer to your question is no, I don't want Kevin Costner."

"Why not?"

"He's a married man."

"Not even in your fantasies?" Anthony persisted, his rich voice dropping low and suggestive.

Her fingers were back toying with the silver disk. "My fantasies don't run to Kevin Costner, no."

Anthony leaned forward, putting both feet on the floor in an open stance, resting his hands on his knees as he asked, "What *do* your fantasies run to, Nikki?" The look in his eyes said she'd walked right into a carefully baited trap.

And, although she knew she'd put him off balance at first, it was obvious to her that he now thought he had her where he wanted her—right in his sights.

Nicole leaned forward, copying his stance.

The movement caused a slight gap in the plunging front of her jacket. The contour of her unrestrained breasts beneath the washed-silk fabric had a devastating effect on his concentration. She knew he couldn't really see anything, but his imagination was on overload. And she was having fun pretending to be someone else.

While he squirmed, she asked, "Have you had a stress test recently, Mr. Gawain?"

"It's Anthony—and no, I haven't. Why?"

"Because without one I think it would be ill-advised for me to go into my fantasies," she informed him with a cat-in-the-cream smile.

"Perhaps I should tell you mine, then," he countered, not letting her slip from his hook so easily.

The studio audience responded with cheers, hoots and shouts of encouragement.

"There's really no need, Anthony. I'm sure I can guess," she answered, nonplused.

"Can you?" He rubbed his chin thoughtfully. "I think I'd like to hear your guess. And I'm sure our studio audience would like to hear it."

The studio audience voiced their agreement.

He settled back on the sofa, his smile a Rhett Butler gauntlet thrown down in response to her femme-fatale challenge. And there was no doubt in anyone's mind that what Nicole Hart was conducting was a flirtation worthy of Miss Scarlett herself.

Nicole was unprepared for this turn of events, but she was unwilling to back down. On the hot seat, she searched her mind for just the right scenario. Finding that hard to do on-camera, she searched for any scenario at all.

Rafe came to mind, and she quickly pieced together what a dream date for him would be. After all, a Lothario was a Lothario was a Lothario....

Taking a deep breath, she began, "Okay, you start out by picking up, say...Kim Basinger."

The audience howled, and Anthony said, "Touché."

"Then what?" he coaxed.

"Dinner. Let's see, you'd probably want to go somewhere you could be seen, but not bothered. Say Dominick's, where you could sneak in the back door and have a steak and fries."

"Okay, not a bad start..." Anthony agreed. "I pick up Miss Basinger in my Ferrari Testarossa coupe and we have an early dinner at Dominick's."

"You have a Ferrari?"

"No. I drive a Jeep four-wheel drive. But it's a fantasy, remember. I thought I'd be sporting and give you some help with the embellishments."

"You *would* pick a testosterone car."

"Testarossa," he said evenly.

"Whatever."

"Okay, we've had dinner. Then what?"

"Hmm..." Nicole stuck her finger in her mouth while she pretended to think. She had his full attention when she offered up, "I know—a Lakers game."

Anthony nodded, if somewhat reluctantly. "Pretty good, pretty good."

She smiled, relieved she'd gotten off the hook so easily.

"Then what?"

"What?"

"You know." He sat forward. "What happens after the Lakers game. It's still early, and I'm a young man—

comparatively." The sexy sparkle in his eyes signaled exactly what he was getting at.

The audience cheered his audacity.

Nicole swallowed. It was her turn to squirm. Oh, dear, how had she let him maneuver her into this spot? More important, how was she going to get out of it? She crossed her legs and resettled herself, playing for time, trying all the while not to notice the young cameraman's interested smirk.

"Yes, we're waiting...." Anthony was baiting her, encouraging the audience's responding shouts of agreement.

And then the gods handed her a reprieve. A way to give her tormentor what he was asking for, though not exactly what he was expecting. She folded her hands calmly and smiled. "Actually, it isn't all that hard to figure, Anthony. Your fantasy would have to end with Miss Basinger fixing you breakfast, of course."

"Oh... Nice euphemism!"

"Thank you." Nicole settled back on the sofa with a quiet sigh of relief.

"I didn't think sex therapists did that...."

Now what was he talking about? Nicole wondered, her guard back up. "Did what?" she asked, looking at him hesitantly, wondering if she'd blown her scam.

His tongue toyed with the inside of his cheek. "You know—used euphemisms."

"They do when they're on television," she answered, relaxing.

"Speaking of television, my producer is signaling it's time to break for commercial."

Nicole turned to watch the monitor where the commercial ran while the producer joined them, checking something with Anthony, clearly not recognizing her as a guest he'd bumped. When the producer walked away after giving Nicole a wink and a circled thumb-and-forefinger "Doing great" sign, Anthony spoke.

"You want to clue me in on what's going on here?"

"Excuse me?"

"You know, Nikki, why you're baiting me?"

"Live in five . . . four . . . three . . . two . . . one," the producer called out.

Anthony looked into the camera. "We're back. In case you're tuning in late—and shame on you if you are—our guest today is sex therapist Nicole Hart." He turned to face her. "So tell us, Nikki, if women don't want men, as you indicated earlier in the show—" he used his hands to convey confusion "—tell us, what *do* women want?"

"You've misunderstood me, Anthony. I didn't say that women don't want men. They do. But it's the nineties—a time when hopefully more women are becoming self-sufficient. It follows that when men are no longer considered a necessity for survival, they become a luxury."

"A luxury?"

Nicole nodded. "Yes, rather like that flashy sports car you covet. Something you don't need, but want just for the thrills it can give you."

The audience went wild applauding her comment.

"Boy, you *are* big on metaphors, aren't you?" Anthony teased when the audience settled back down.

"I'm not the one lusting after a flashy sports car," she retorted, her dark eyes bright with sexual innuendo as she moistened her lips.

"I promise we'll get to what you lust after in a moment," he answered on a rich laugh.

That retort scored points with the audience—and with Nicole. It displayed his ability to take having his image pricked.

Nicole smiled at his implied threat. He might be a male chauvinist pig, she decided, but at least he wasn't a male chauvinist *prig*.

Anthony cleared his throat. "If I understand you correctly now, you're saying men are a luxury for today's women. That men are no longer the number-one item on the list of woman's wants."

Nicole nodded, ready to mix research and personal opinion.

"That's correct. Women are slowly moving into the position of being able to make choices based less on what they need and more on what they desire. They can, for instance, begin to choose a partner based on personal preferences, rather than the traditional reason—economic security for herself and any children she might want to have.

"In other words, women are finally becoming able to choose their partners with the same degree of personal indulgence that men have always enjoyed. And it goes without saying, that freedom also includes the ability to make the same colossal mistakes that can be made when a choice is made by caprice."

"What about women who want to stay home? Women who want to raise their own children and keep a home full-time, women who want a more traditional life and don't want a career outside the home?"

"I think that's a great choice, too. But not without the protection they are finally being guaranteed to help them survive abandonment, divorce, or the death of a spouse."

"Okay, so we've established times are changing. What I want to know is, if a man isn't the first item on a woman's shopping list any longer, then what is? In the nineties, what do women want?"

"Chocolate," Nikki answered. She was a confirmed chocoholic.

"I'm serious, Nikki."

"So am I. I'd do most anything for a bag of chocolate M&M's candies."

Anthony's dark eyebrow lifted. "And here I'm fresh out. What's the big deal with women and chocolate, anyway?"

"Studies have shown chocolate gives the same rush as sexual desire. And there are no dirty socks to pick up, no toothpaste squeezed in the middle, no toilet seats left up," she said. She was on a roll now.

"You don't like men much at all, do you?"

Nicole's shrug was casually dismissive. "Oh, they do have their uses. They're good for an extra paycheck and a quick toss, I suppose—with an emphasis on the quick."

Anthony turned to the audience with a look of consternation. He shook his head at their laughter. When it subsided, he informed them, "Uh-uh, not me. I'm not touching that line." Turning back to Nicole, he said, "Okay, you've stated that women have this mysterious thing for chocolate because of its supposed ability to give them some libidinous kick. But after chocolate, what do women want? What is it they crave and aren't getting from men?"

"You haven't any idea? A man the Entertainment News section of the L.A. *Times* says has a legendary prowess with women?" Nicole teased.

There was a chorus of impressed "whoas" from the audience.

Anthony groaned. "If I were you, Nikki, I wouldn't believe everything I read."

"I don't," she replied, further disconcerting him and keeping the audience animated.

"Flowers," Anthony said, obviously wanting to move ahead and away from discussing himself. "Flowers must rate pretty high with women."

"Flowers are nice," Nicole agreed. "But practical women of the nineties prefer something that lasts longer than a bouquet of flowers."

"Diamonds, right?"

"Is that a proposal, Anthony?" she asked flirtatiously.

"No. If I were proposing something, I'd buy you a giant bag of M&M's."

That got the laugh he wanted from the audience, and even a half smile from Nicole. "Now, back to my question," he continued. "Lets leave chocolate, flowers and other sundry romantic items by the wayside and get to men and women specifically. What would you say was the main thing women want from men and aren't getting?"

"Do you like rock-and-roll music, Anthony?" Her question brought a look of surprise to his face.

"Sure, why?"

"Then perhaps you're a Rolling Stones fan...."

"I like the Stones...."

"Then maybe you can tell me the title of one of their biggest hits."

"They've had a lot of hits."

"This is a fairly early one."

"You don't mean—?"

"That's right. 'I can't get no satisfaction,' as Mick Jagger would say."

"Satisfaction, eh? And I guess sexual satisfaction is something a sex therapist like yourself would know an intimidating lot about."

It was clear he thought he'd turned the tables on her, but she was having none of it. "You don't have to be a sex therapist to know men are obsessed with speed," she said. "And not just when it comes to flashy sports cars, either.

"It's hardly a secret that men are too quick—too quick with the actual sex act, and too quick to turn over and fall asleep afterward."

The audience was so quiet you could have heard a cotton ball drop.

Anthony cleared his throat.

That caused a tittering to sweep the audience.

"What...what do you suppose it is that... Ah, why do you suppose men are so quick?" Anthony finally managed to ask. "Is it because men are insensitive brutes? Is that what you're getting at?"

"No..."

"No?"

"Well, some are, of course. But I don't think insensitivity is the main reason."

"Okay, we're not insensitive brutes, guys," Anthony said, looking to the audience to include them. "Well, if we're not insensitive brutes—then what? Are we uneducated about women and what they desire when it comes to sex? Is that what you're saying, Nikki?"

He really thought he was cute, sitting there, all gorgeous-male-specimen making a pretense at being one with the men in the audience, most of whom didn't rank within a stone's throw of him in masculine assurance. She didn't feel a bit guilty about her charade.

Nicole shook her head and plunged ahead. "There has been too much media attention on the subject for that to be possible. I think most men know women want foreplay and want it to last as long as—"

"An egg timer," Anthony interjected with a wide, sexy grin.

Nicole just looked at him. "No, more like a football quarter."

Nicole's byplay brought the females in the audience to their feet, cheering and clapping.

"The visiting team scores an extra point," Anthony said wryly.

"An extra point? I didn't know we were keeping score," Nicole muttered.

"Like hell you didn't," Anthony whispered back as the audience settled down.

"Okay, if I understand you correctly, Nikki, you're saying that lack of education on the part of the male isn't the problem. You believe men know what women want, they just aren't delivering it—for whatever reason."

"That's right."

"So, bottom line, why aren't men delivering what women want? What is the problem? Are men just plain selfish?"

"Some men may be, but in my opinion the reason the majority of men omit or only give token attention to the foreplay they know women want and/or require for a fully satisfying sexual experience is that they are afraid of the consequences—or I should say the possible consequences—of not doing so." Maybe she should be an actress, she thought. She was pretty good.

"The consequences? I'm afraid you've lost me, Nikki. I don't understand."

"Think about it. Wouldn't you agree men assume that women measure their desirability to them by their erection?" She amazed herself. She hadn't even blushed.

Anthony nodded, his green eyes looking a little skittish. He didn't comment, however; just waited silently for her to get to wherever she was heading in order to make her point.

She obliged him by continuing. "And a man measures how desirable he is by his erection...."

Anthony just kept nodding, remaining silent, but swallowing visibly.

"So what's the logical problem, then?" she asked, knowing full well Anthony wasn't prepared in any way to answer the question, and loving every torturous second of his discomfort.

"You tell me," he choked out.

"That's easy. Men are afraid."

"Afraid? Of what?"

"Afraid the longer the period of time that elapses, the greater the danger they will lose their ability to sustain their erection. And as we all know, there is only one word more frightening to men than the word *commitment*. Can you say *impotent?*"

"No, can't say as that word is in my vocabulary."

Nicole shot him a look and a one-word challenge: "Yet."

The audience went wild, applauding their standoff, as the producer signaled that they were out of time.

NICOLE PULLED HER WHITE sports car out of traffic and parked.

Unwinding from behind the wheel of the splashy, though inexpensive, car, she smiled. What, she wondered, would Anthony Gawain say if he could see her sports car, after the grief she'd given him about lusting after one?

Her smile turned into a grimace as her headache returned full force, reminding her why she'd stopped at Vons. Pulling off the charade of being a sex therapist had been fun, but trying.

The whole ordeal had given her a stress headache that required extra-strength aspirin and gave new meaning to the pet name she'd given him—Gawain the Pain. Accomplishing her goal of getting on "The Anthony Gawain Show" and giving him a hard time had been very satisfying. Now her head was presenting her with the check for the pleasure.

A few minutes after ducking into Vons, she was back in her car and heading home, her head still pounding. After pulling out into traffic, she'd tried without success to wrench the childproof cap from the bottle of aspirin, enduring several horn blasts and rude gestures from passing motorists enraged by her erratic maneuvering.

She gave up when she realized she didn't have any liquid to take the tablets with. She was such a baby about pills, and there was no way she could swallow one without something to wash it down with. Driving until she spotted a Ralph's, she pulled over and parked again to get some bottled water.

While she stood in line at the checkout with the bottled water, she massaged her temple and ran through the show once again in her mind. She had had Anthony Gawain on the ropes, at least until the end of the show, when he'd rallied and their sparring had ended in a draw. Had her charade really been as successful as she thought?

Rafe would tell her.

Though he was years younger, he mothered her. Which was pretty funny, as men didn't come much more macho than Rafe Contreras.

The checker ran up her bottled water, and Nicole added a bag of M&M's on impulse, as well as an L.A. *Times.*

Back at her car, she opened the tablets and washed one down with several swallows of the bottled water. By the time she had stopped at home and changed into something more casual for her shift at Le Bistro, her headache had subsided.

She felt like Cinderella when she put the outfit she'd worn in the closet. It wasn't that she didn't dress up herself, it was only that the persona she'd assumed had been so daring.

Rafe was waiting for her in the employees' lounge when she arrived at Le Bistro. "Good job, lady. You turned him every which way but loose," he said with open admiration.

"Really? I really did?" She couldn't hide her pleasure at his assessment.

"I bet the ratings go through the roof and he'll have to ask you back. And the sex-therapist stuff—even I was buying it. You really sounded like you knew what you were talking about."

Nicole laughed. "I'll be back on that show over Anthony Gawain's dead body. I may have gotten around his smarmy producer, but I didn't exactly make a conquest of Gawain the Swain. By the end of the show, he was more than glad to see me go."

"I wouldn't be too sure about that," Rafe told her. "His body language said he wanted to eat you up with a spoon—or maybe turn you over his knee. You cooked his goose but good, lady."

"I got to him, then?"

"In spades. Trust me on that."

"Good." Her revenge was sweet.

"How do you know I got to him?" Nicole was embarrassed to hear herself ask the question. Rafe would think she was a total idiot when it came to men. Unfortunately, she was afraid a lot of the time she was. It would have been so helpful to have had a male influence growing up. As it was, she felt like she was dealing with aliens when it came to men. And when she was attracted to them, they were even more unfathomable.

"Oh, you got to Gawain, all right," Rafe assured her. "He's a pretty cool customer when it comes to being in control of the interview. But you made him lose control. Remember, he promised to get back to what you lust after? Well, he forgot." Rafe winked. "But I promise you, he's thinking about it now."

"Oh, Rafe."

"I'm serious, lady," he said, plucking the L.A. *Times* from her hand. Turning to the movie section, he scanned the page. "Want to go to the movies tonight to celebrate your success?" he asked without looking up.

He was mothering her again. Nicole arched an eyebrow. "*You* don't have a *date?*"

"I want to see *The Last of the Mohicans*, and I don't want to take a date."

"Why not?"

"She'll drool over Daniel Day-Lewis, and I do so hate damp popcorn."

"I don't know, Rafe. Daniel Day-Lewis is pretty high on my drool meter."

"So you'll buy your own popcorn." Rafe set the newspaper down. "Time to go to work."

"Rafe . . ."

He stopped on his way out of the lounge and looked back at her.

"Thanks."

"Don't thank me, lady. You did good. I promise, you haven't seen the last of Anthony Gawain."

"I'd better have. I mean, after all, Rafe, scamming as a sex therapist for one show is one thing, but I couldn't possibly keep up the charade. I got my revenge, and that's all I wanted from getting on the show. I don't know why you think he hasn't already forgotten who I am."

"Well, for one thing, you got to him. But that wasn't the worst of it. The worst of it was that you battled him to a draw. Men like clear victories, you know. And you did it in front of an audience, which is even more galling. Trust me, it's gonna bug him until he gets a chance to win a clear-cut victory over you."

As Nicole watched Rafe leave the lounge, she shook her head.

He was a little late with his warning.

Anthony Gawain had already settled the score. While he'd appeared intrigued with her, he hadn't made a pass. Though she would have rebuffed him, she couldn't help feeling more than a little rejected—and supremely annoyed with herself for feeling that way.

She thought of her mother and two sisters, who looked like triplets. If only she were beautiful like they were. All three of them were blond, blue-eyed, all-American cheerleader types, with dimples to boot.

She, on the other hand, had average-brown hair and eyes. Her mother had always insisted she looked exotic, but Nicole didn't feel anything but plain next to the three of them.

The only way she'd been able to even attempt to pull off the seductive act for the Anthony Gawain Show was because it had been just that—an act. She'd *assumed* the part, pretending she was beautiful and desirable.

In real life she had no confidence in her appearance.

And with men, appearance was what counted. Every survey or study she'd ever come across in a magazine confirmed that every man on the planet wanted a beautiful, sexy woman to decorate his arm. It was how he was judged by the world, and how he judged his own worth, as well.

And while it annoyed her to be rejected by Anthony Gawain, it annoyed her even more that she was attracted to him. Had she inherited her mother's weakness for men who would always leave? Her mother, with all her beauty, had never been able to hold a man's continuing interest, so how could she hope to?

If she were interested—and she wasn't—she couldn't pick a man more impossible to hold than Anthony Gawain.

The talk-show host might be hip, smug and arrogant, but he was no fool. Talk shows brought in big bucks, mostly because they were cheap to produce. His audience was young and attractive to advertisers.

Unlike other talk-show hosts, Anthony Gawain didn't scramble for famous guests. He didn't pander to his audience, either. His show was about ideas, not people. He had brains. His bottom-line appeal was the fact that he was a high-IQ rebel with a strong sense of the absurd. He was every inch the wandering knight in search of the truth.

In other words, if she were trying, she couldn't find a better blind date from hell for herself.

And while she might be attracted to Anthony Gawain, she knew enough to steer clear of his particular brand of heartbreak.

Rafe was wrong. Anthony Gawain would never call her.

She told herself it didn't matter, because she wouldn't agree to see him again if he did call.

How could she?

She wasn't a sex therapist.

She wasn't even sexy.

But it had been exciting to pretend.

# 3

*Los Angeles Times*

Entertainment News:

ITEM . . . Everyone is still talking about Gawain the Swain and the sexy sex therapist who rocked him back on his heels. That particular show in the What Do Women Want? series kicked his ratings into the stratosphere. This columnist wonders if Anthony Gawain will be seeing more of the sexy sex therapist.

ANTHONY GAWAIN scowled at the newspaper in his hand.

The columnist was creating something from thin air again, just as she'd created the reputation as a ladies' man that had gained him such a wide audience.

His grin was rueful as he pictured Nicole Hart . . . "the sexy sex therapist." Well, maybe his favorite columnist hadn't fabricated the item *completely* from thin air, he admitted to himself, tossing down the newspaper and heading for the shower.

He looked at his face in the bathroom mirror.

A late night at Roxbury, the hot club of the hour, showed in his half-shuttered eyes and stubbled chin. He hadn't left his booth all night, had just sat watching the dancing while the pounding music numbed his mind. He hadn't gone to the VIP Room. His ego didn't need it.

Shrugging out of his navy robe in his high-tech bathroom of gray granite, chrome, and white tile, he continued to think of Nicole Hart. The loud music and the shots of Jack Daniel's bourbon hadn't gotten her off his mind. The columnist was right about her being sexy, and he'd been attracted to her mightily.

But she was a little too glib for his taste.

When it came down to it, he preferred a woman he could really talk with. A woman who listened and participated rather than performed. Even though Nicole Hart's performance had been very stimulating in its way.

Sometimes he wished he were the sort of man who didn't think so much, wished he could take things at face value without looking for the truth. The sort of man who saw everything in black-and-white, didn't notice the shadings of gray.

He'd rebelled against his political family and the image of perfection they'd wanted him to uphold. At an early age he'd learned about half-truths and damage control, and he'd hated it.

The truth was all that mattered to him. It couldn't hurt the way lies could. And the truth was the appeal of his shocking TV talk show.

He knew all about women like Nicole Hart. Like most women, she wanted a man she could dupe. She'd even said as much, with her "extra paycheck and quick toss" lines. No. Nicole Hart wasn't for him. What he wanted was a simple, uncomplicated woman without a hidden agenda—if such a woman existed.

Turning the water on full blast, he stepped into the oversize shower stall. The steamy mist swirled around him, fogging the glass enclosure. The tile floor was cool beneath his feet while the hot water rained stinging drops against his skin. He stretched, letting the water sluice down his lean frame to form rivulets through his hair. Then he quickly finished his shower using a bar of milled soap subtly scented with his favorite designer aroma.

Forty-five minutes later, he was at Patrick's Roadhouse for his weekly breakfast meeting with Mark.

"You're late," Mark said as Anthony slid into the chair opposite him. "I took the liberty of ordering your usual."

"All I want is coffee, and lots of it," Anthony growled. He ignored the copy of the L.A. *Times* lying folded in the middle of the table. Mark had opened it to the column in the Entertainment News.

"Did you see the column?" Mark asked.

Anthony nodded.

"So, are you?" Mark asked as the waitress brought their order and set it down on the table before them.

"Could you bring us a pot of coffee for the table?" Anthony requested.

The waitress nodded and quickly returned with it. When she'd ascertained that there were no other requests, she left them to their breakfast.

"Well, are you going to see more of the sex therapist?" Mark persisted.

"Are you working for the columnist now?" Anthony asked, nodding at the newspaper.

"No, just curious. The two of you seemed to hit it off pretty well."

"Where'd you find her?" Anthony asked, avoiding answering.

Mark shrugged. "Someone called in a favor from someone. All I know is, I was given her name."

Anthony considered Mark's reply as he drained his cup of coffee and poured a fresh one.

"Oh, that reminds me," Mark added. "You need to call your agent."

"Why? Was the series such a success the network is begging me to take more money?"

"No, an editor from some publishing company called the studio requesting your agent's name and phone number."

"Boy, they sure take it personal when you don't rejoin their book club," Anthony said dryly.

"They want you to join their book club, all right, but as an author. They want you to write a book."

Anthony sighed, pushing his uneaten omelet away. "How long is it going to take these publishers to understand I'm not interested in their offers to write a tell-all book about my family?"

Mark swallowed a bite of his French toast, shaking his head. "They aren't interested in you writing a book about your family. They want you to write a book based on the sweeps-week series. And you might want to make a point of seeing more of the sexy sex therapist, because they want her to coauthor it with you."

"You're kidding!" Anthony was taken aback by the news.

Mark shook his head no as the waitress returned with a cordless phone. "Call for you, Mr. Gawain," she said, handing him the phone.

Answering it, Anthony heard his agent repeat the offer, also naming the amount the publisher had offered as an advance—an amount so obscenely generous that even his high-powered agent sounded giddy.

"Does Miss Hart know about this?" Anthony asked.

"No. I thought it might be good for you to approach her first."

"I'll take care of it and get back to you," Anthony said, hanging up.

He didn't think it was a good idea to tell Nicole Hart straight out. He'd have to build up to it, make her want to work with him—which he didn't think was possible at the moment. He'd gotten the distinct impression that she didn't really like him, despite her flirting.

IT WAS A WARM, BREEZY night as Anthony walked through the narrow passageway leading from the tree-lined garden of Sofi's Patio Restaurant.

One of the advantages of growing up in his wealthy family had been the series of chefs his family employed, giving him an appreciation of fine food. Fortunately, the Oriental discipline of karate kept his body honed, despite his love of the pleasures of the table.

Tonight, Greek ballads had played softly in the background while he'd been served his favorite pastitsio, one of Sofi's clientele's favorite dishes. It rivaled the rice-stuffed tomatoes, which one had to order in advance.

Anthony was in a very satisfied mood as he left the restaurant and pulled his Jeep into traffic and left west Hollywood. Nikki was the only troubling thought on his mind.

How was he going to find a way to work with this woman who didn't even like him?

He was a loner—even in a crowd of people. It wasn't that he didn't have social skills; it was that he used them to keep his distance. He participated without becoming involved—with family, friends, women, business associates.

But lately he'd been confused. He'd begun to question some of the beliefs he'd formed early in life. Maybe he was maturing, beginning to see life in a different way. Was it possible he needed people to care about, to care about him? He was beginning to figure out that he wasn't so much bored as lonely.

Driving and shifting gears with a race driver's ease, he imagined Nikki, the woman who'd put her name on the solution to his loneliness. He imagined her as his dinner companion.

As he drove, the traffic thinned out, allowing him the luxury of his fantasy. The warm, soft breeze fingered his long hair as he pictured Nicole Hart sitting across from him at dinner, smelling as good as the fresh flowers at Sofi's.

What would she have worn to taunt him this time? he wondered. A rakish grin tilted the corners of his mouth as he decided. She would have worn the outfit L.A.'s leading female designer was pushing this year— a navy pin-striped minisuit over a black lace bustier.

Her shoes—what kind of shoes did he want her to wear? He mentally went through her closet until he found a pair of strappy black mules in softest leather. He laughed as he thought of the sudden foot fetish Nikki provoked in him.

Nicole Hart gave him an incredible case of the nibbles. He very much wanted to nibble her toes, her earlobes, her inner thighs....

He shook his head to clear it and turned on the radio to distract himself. Garth Brooks was belting out an anthem to the alpha male brought to his knees by a woman. Finding the lyrics a little too close for comfort, he fiddled with the buttons, passing on Metallica in favor of a popular nighttime talk show.

"Okay, you ladies out there in radio land, I'm taking the last call for your vote on The Sexiest Man Alive survey we're conducting here tonight. After I take this call, we'll have a commercial break, and our guest will then answer your questions about your love life.

"Now back to our survey. So far we've got Kevin Costner leading the pack by two votes."

Anthony couldn't help patting himself on the back for the Kevin Costner vote. He'd been right in suggesting him as what women wanted when Nikki had asked.

"Hello, who do we have on the line?" the deejay asked, breaking into Anthony's thoughts.

"This is Kathy from Santa Monica."

"Well, Kathy, who's the sexiest man alive?"

"Anthony Gawain."

"The talk-show host?"

Anthony shot his radio a dirty look at the deejay's note of surprise.

"Yeah, he's hot."

Starting to feel embarrassed, Anthony reached out to change the station, but stopped when he heard the deejay announce, "We'll be right back with our guest sex therapist after this message."

Could the guest be Nikki? he wondered—no, hoped.

A carful of young girls passed him, honking and waving, as he waited for the commercial break to end.

The sex therapist wasn't Nicole Hart, but he continued to listen anyway.

"What do you think makes a man sexy?" the deejay asked his guest.

"Really liking women as a sex," the therapist answered. "What do *you* think makes a woman sexy?"

"Well, breathing is always good," the deejay said, going for a laugh, but not getting it. "Okay, ah, the way she walks."

"Yes, a woman's walk can denote power and confidence."

"Ah, yes . . ." The deejay was clearly out of his league, and Anthony sympathized with him. "Let's take some calls from our listeners and see what's on their minds, why don't we? The number is 555-9999."

After a few seconds, the deejay took the first call.

"Hello, you're on KTIX talk radio. Tell us your name and the question you have for our guest tonight.

"This is Bob. I was wondering, what kinda degree do you got to have to be a sex therapist? It sounds like a pretty cushy job to me."

"To practice, you need a lot of schooling, Bob. I have a masters degree and a Ph.D. and I had to serve a two-year apprenticeship," the therapist replied.

Nikki had hardly looked old enough to have completed that much education, Anthony mused before being distracted by the next caller's question.

"I'm confused," a caller identifying herself as Chelsea said. "I didn't know there was a difference between being attractive and being sexy. Could you explain what you were talking about earlier?"

The therapist cleared her throat. "Attractiveness, physical appearance, is about how you look, and to some extent it can be achieved cosmetically. 'Sexy,' however, comes from within. It's about how you feel concerning your self-image. It's a glow that comes from inside—an attitude."

As Anthony turned his Jeep off the Pacific Coast highway for his home in Malibu, he thought about the book-contract offer.

It had come at the perfect time. He needed a challenge. And something told him getting Nicole Hart to agree to coauthor it was going to be a challenge. Of course, he didn't plan to admit to anyone that he was writing a book—what if he couldn't pull it off?

What if his father was right in his assessment that he would never amount to anything in the long run? That the talk show had been only lucky happenstance?

What if he couldn't repeat his success?

With his famous name, there would be nowhere to hide if the book was a failure.

# 4

ALL NICOLE WANTED was to go to bed. She was exhausted after staying up half the night working on her screenplay and then working a busy shift at Le Bistro.

"Are you sure you know how to do this?" she asked, opening the front door of the cottage. She shouldn't have complained about the dripping shower head keeping her awake at night, because Rafe had insisted on following her home to fix it.

"No problem," Rafe assured her. He headed for the bathroom, waving his wrench like a warrior's sword. The blinking green light on her answering machine signaled that someone had called and left a message. She hoped it was an agent who was interested in representing her, but she quickly replaced that expectation with a more realistic one—it was more likely a message left by some computer-generated sales pitch.

Six months of knocking on doors, leaving messages, fending passes, had netted her zilch. The legitimate producers, directors and studios all had an army of personnel to keep them from being bothered. They were virtually impossible to reach without contacts.

You needed an agent just to get someone to agree to look at your work, and an agent usually only wanted someone who'd already sold something.

And there were the bottom feeders—the jerks who used their positions to liven up their personal lives. Mark Bates had been the latest one to frustrate her pursuit of success.

She pushed the play button on her answering machine.

"Hello, Ms. Hart. This is Central Casting. We have some movie-extra work for you. Please call the agency if you're available."

Nicole knew she'd return the call. Not for the ninety dollars a day movie-extra work paid—although she could use it—but for the contacts she might make on the movie set. She knew Rafe would trade hours with her to accommodate her schedule.

As she laid her keys next to the pot of ivy on the white wooden mantel, the answering machine beeped and spat out a second message—a message that caused her to sink down onto the sofa in stunned surprise.

"Hello, Nikki. This is Anthony." There was a long pause, then, "Ah, Anthony Gawain. The thing is, I've got these two tickets to a Garth Brooks concert. I'll call you back later this evening."

Nicole sat staring dumbly at the answering machine, listening to the whir of the tape rewinding. Finally she closed her gaping mouth and yelled for Rafe to join her.

"What? What is it?" he asked, responding to the anxiety in her voice.

"Listen to this." She reached to press the play button on the machine.

Rafe's body tensed, and his eyes narrowed. "What is it? An obscene phone call?"

"You could say that."

The message from Central Casting played back.

"I don't get it," Rafe said.

"No, not that message. This one." The machine beeped, and Anthony's voice filled the room.

A big smile wreathed Rafe's face as he relaxed. "I told you so."

"You don't have to sound so smug about it. And you can wipe that stupid grin off your face. I'm not going."

"You gotta be kidding! Do you know how hard it is to get tickets to a Garth Brooks concert? Hell, I'll go if you won't."

"Good. When he calls back later, you can tell him that."

"Uh-uh. As soon as I get your shower head fixed, I'm leaving. I've got a hot date." Heading back to the bathroom, while Nicole sulked, he called out, "That's *date*. It's an interesting concept, dating. You ought to try it."

Nicole threw a ruffled pillow from the sofa in his direction.

He laughed and ducked into the bathroom.

A half hour later, he was finished fixing her plumbing problem and came out of the bathroom to find her dozing on the sofa. Leno was doing his monologue on the TV. Rafe turned off the set and was trying to decide whether to wake Nicole or just settle her more comfortably on the sofa when the phone rang.

He picked it up.

It was Anthony Gawain.

"I'm the plumber," Rafe answered in response to his question. "Ms. Hart isn't in, but she left word for you that she'd love to attend the concert you called about. Would you like me to leave her a message from you when I finish up my repairs here?"

Hanging up the phone a few seconds later, Rafe scribbled down Anthony's instructions. A quick glance assured him that Nicole was still asleep on the sofa. He left the message by the phone, and went to settle her more comfortably, deciding to take the coward's way out and not wake her.

She was going to kill him, he thought, looking down at her.

But not if he wasn't around.

Later, when she cooled down, he'd find a way to convince her he'd only been trying to help her. That he'd made the date for her with Anthony Gawain for her own good.

He let himself out and whistled as he walked to his car, much like someone whistling as he walked past a graveyard.

SHE WAS GOING TO KILL Rafe Contreras.

Fuming, Nicole jerked a pair of jeans—the very ones Rafe had coaxed her into buying two weeks ago at Dungarees on Ventura—from their hanger.

She hadn't been able to reach Anthony Gawain or Rafe the Rat by phone, so she was trapped into being ready for the date with Anthony when he arrived.

Tucking her white T-shirt into the jeans, she glanced in the mirror above the painted dresser. She hoped she wasn't dressed too casually. And what was she going to do with her hair?

She could cheerfully strangle Rafe for not even being here when she needed him. He'd been a tremendous help getting her ready for her charade on "The Anthony Gawain Show," not only helping her pick out what to wear, but also complimenting her until she'd actually felt sexy—well, sort of, anyway....

Every woman should have her own personal dresser. She had no doubt Rafe was going to make it big as a costume designer in Hollywood someday— if she let him live.

Meanwhile, she had to do something with her hair, she thought, rolling up the short sleeves of her T-shirt. She slipped on a wide silver cuff bracelet and hunted down her silver cactus earrings, ever mindful of the time sliding by. She'd had the whole day to get ready, as it was her day off, but she'd been too daunted by the prospect of actually going out on a bona fide date with the sexy talk-show host to get her act together until the last minute.

Buckling the narrow leather belt she'd pushed through the loops of her jeans, she scanned the message Rafe had left her. Yes, he'd written four o'clock as the time Anthony had designated to pick her up. Why Anthony was arriving at four in the afternoon for a concert date wasn't explained. Perhaps he planned for them to eat an early dinner beforehand. Maybe he planned to take her to Dominick's out of spite.

Bending from the waist, she pulled on a pair of low-cut white cowboy boots she'd bought last season, hopping on one foot and then the other.

There. She was dressed.

Except her vest, she remembered. On her way to the closet, she stopped to check her makeup in the mirror—and freaked.

Her hair! She'd forgotten about doing her hair!

She glanced at the digital clock on the bedside table. It was already four o'clock. There was nothing to do but slick her hair straight back with styling gel and hope for the best.

What could Rafe have been thinking, pulling such a stunt? she wondered, pooling gel in her palm. She was going to have to continue her charade as a sex therapist for a whole evening, not just a half-hour talk show.

Maybe she should just tell Anthony the truth. Naw . . . she wasn't feeling that brave at the moment. If the subject came up, she'd steer the conversation to a safer topic. They could talk about— Oh, dear, what *could* they talk about?

The only thing they'd talked about on his show was sex.

Was that why he'd asked her out? She slid her hands through her hair, styling it. Was Anthony expecting her to be the hot number she'd pretended to be on his show? Surely no one expected *that* on a first date in the changed social scene of the nineties.

Her occasional dates weren't a very good point of reference. The guys she dated weren't the type to brave much beyond a good-night kiss. Rafe was right about her beaux.

Anthony clearly didn't fall into that classification.

Anthony Gawain was one-hundred-percent adult male on the prowl. A heartthrob. Thanks to Rafe, she was going out on a date with a man who was way too exciting to be legal.

On top of which she was very much afraid she wasn't up to Anthony's speed, she thought, washing the gel off her hands as the doorbell pealed.

Oh, well, maybe for one night she could pretend.

She went to the door and opened it.

"At least I'm dressed all right," she said with relief when she saw what Anthony wore.

"I'd say better than all right," Anthony replied, letting his gaze slide over her appreciatively. "What would you say to staying in and ordering pizza?" His eyes were all dark, sexy invitation.

"What about Garth Brooks?" she asked, ignoring his suggestion.

"Let him get his own pizza."

"I mean the concert," she said, patiently.

"What would you say if I didn't really have tickets to a Garth Brooks concert?" he asked.

"Good night," she answered, starting to close the door.

He quickly reached into his pocket and produced two tickets. "Luckily, I've got proof."

"I'm curious, Anthony. What made you invite me to a concert with you?" Nicole asked, looking at the tickets he waved under her nose.

"Kim Basinger is busy?" he suggested.

She waited.

"I've had a stress test?" he tried again.

She waited.

He waited.

She gave in. "Okay, let's go. You can take me for a fast ride in your Testa-whatever...."

NICOLE JUST BARELY restrained herself from pinching her arm to see if she was indeed dreaming. She was having a great deal of trouble believing she wasn't. And if she wasn't dreaming, then Anthony Gawain gave good date—no, he gave *fantastic* date.

Either Rafe hadn't taken very careful notes or Anthony had deliberately omitted a few details about his proposed "date." While it was true the talk-show host had invited her to attend a Garth Brooks concert— that much Rafe had gotten right—there'd been no mention that the concert wasn't in L.A., or even in the state of California.

It was in Dallas, Texas!

And she'd been right about them having an early dinner before the concert—she just hadn't dreamed it would be on an airplane.

After they'd landed in Dallas several hours later, it had taken them twenty minutes just to limo out of the sprawling D-FW airport and head for the concert at Reunion Arena.

Conversation hadn't been the problem she'd expected. They'd exchanged pleasantries about the weather, L.A. traffic and country music on the ride to the airport, but once they'd boarded the plane and been airborne, he'd promptly fallen asleep.

She'd been both mortified and relieved.

A date falling asleep on her wouldn't be something to write in her diary about—if she kept one. Rafe would howl when she told him about it.

Maybe she wouldn't tell him.

She'd let the stewardess awaken him for the meal. He'd apologized then, explaining he'd taken an allergy medication. She wasn't at all sure she believed him.

In fact, while he'd slept, she'd begun to wonder if he hadn't somehow discovered the scam she'd pulled on him and this date was some hoax he was pulling off on her as payback. Why else would he have this sudden interest in dating her? Sure, there'd been a great chemistry between them on his show, but he hadn't followed up on it when he'd had the opportunity afterward. Either he was getting even, or he wanted something. All she could do was wait to see which.

At the moment, he was on the limo's car phone with his producer about a snag in an upcoming show. She glanced over at him, studying him covertly. He was wearing a white shirt unbuttoned at the throat, lived-in jeans, and cowboy boots. His taste in cowboy boots was as unconventional as his taste in ties; the boots were black with a red, green and blue design scrawled on them.

As the limo made its way through traffic to the entrance to Reunion Arena, Nicole wondered what Anthony Gawain was like in bed. Was the talk-show host a talker, or a silent lover? Did he let his hair down from that ponytail—?

"What are you thinking about?" Anthony asked, his deep, sexy voice catching her off guard in the intimacy of the limo. He'd finished his conversation while she'd been lost in thought.

"I'm—I—" she stammered. "You never said why you asked me out." No way was she going to give him the satisfaction of knowing she'd been thinking sexy thoughts about him.

"You seemed to have a lot to say about women's desires when you were on my show. I thought perhaps we could explore the topic further. . . ."

"What, are you writing a book?" she asked flippantly, disappointed by his answer. Had she really been expecting him to say he was attracted to her, found her attractive? She needed to get a grip on reality. Anthony Gawain had his dance card filled several times over by stunningly beautiful women.

"Maybe," he replied. "What do you think—"

She interrupted him, feeling unaccountably miffed. "I think we covered the subject pretty well on your show."

"No. We covered the fact that you think men are afraid of strong women because we think a strong woman will make us impotent."

"So you're going out with me to prove you aren't impotent?"

"No. I thought maybe if you got to know me you might like me," he answered, his eyes staring into hers.

"Oh." Unable to hold his gaze, she looked away. She was very much afraid that might well be the case. Anthony was the sort of handsome charmer she had her mother's weakness for, the type she avoided the way she avoided shark-infested waters.

She didn't want or need a man like Anthony Gawain in her life. She wanted a permanent relationship with a man, and he was restless seeker, one she couldn't hope to hold.

A smart woman didn't try to hold on to the bright red balloon in the fair of life. A smart woman opted for the cuddly, comforting, teddy bear.

And she was a smart woman.

Wasn't she?

GARTH BROOKS WAS onstage, a single red rose in his hand. Always at his best as a moody torch singer, Garth was giving a heartfelt rendition of his hit single, "Shameless." It was a show-stopping number he'd performed at the CMA Awards. As he sang, he held the women in the audience in the palm of his hand. Anthony looked over to see that Nicole was no exception.

Anthony smiled ruefully. The title of the song was apt where his motives were concerned. He'd been shameless to fly her to this concert to try to impress her first, instead of coming straight out and asking her if she would agree to write a book with him—though he didn't think his falling asleep on the plane had impressed her much.

But she did seem to be enjoying the concert. It was almost impossible not to be carried along on the wave of enthusiasm swelling from the crowd around them.

Garth Brooks mania had packed the arena. He held the crowd in his grip. And it wasn't a sedate concert at all—the exuberant tone of Garth's performance and the flashy staging made it seem more like a rock concert. The performer seemed to be on a personal mission to infuse every person in the audience with the joy he felt in his music.

Holding the long-stemmed red rose, he poured his heart into the lyrics of the song, his knees flexed, his neck straining, his eyes closed.

Anthony couldn't imagine being a man brought to his knees by a woman, as the lyric implied. If that was love, he didn't want any part of it. He wasn't a man like his father—a man who could be duped by a woman. He'd never trust a woman to that degree, and he'd never let one get close enough to destroy him.

Women used the word *love* for leverage. It was a word that came easily to their lips. And the smarter the woman, the more dangerous she was.

Nicole Hart was a very dangerous woman. He'd known it the first time he saw her. She was not only sexy, she was smart—and ready to take him on. Take him down.

Given a choice, he would have steered way clear of her.

But he didn't have a choice.

Not if he wanted to write the book. He'd just have to lock up his heart when he locked up the contract.

The song ended to thunderous applause. Caught up in the moment, he and Nicole surged to their feet.

Strobe lights flashed as Garth took his much-deserved bows.

Nicole was accidentally jostled by a cheering fan next to her. Losing her balance, she fell against Anthony, grabbing hold of him for support.

He reached to steady her. Still holding her in his arms, he looked down at her. "Are you having a good time?"

"What?" she yelled back. His words had been lost in the din of the crowd's cheers when Garth broke into an encore.

Anthony bent down and placed his lips against her ear. "I asked if you were having a good time," he repeated.

She nodded and smiled broadly.

He relaxed. The evening was going as planned.

On the plane ride home—while she was still feeling the glow of the concert—he'd make the coauthoring proposal.

He cupped his hand against her ear. "Do you mind if we duck out now to avoid the rush to the exit in a few minutes? If we don't, I'm afraid we'll get caught up in the crush of traffic and miss our flight back to L.A."

She nodded her agreement, and he took her hand to lead her out to the aisle. Once there, they headed for the entrance and the waiting limo.

Anthony groaned when he saw that his best-laid plans had been pushed aside. Leaving the arena, they were met by a thick, enveloping fog—the kind that kept planes from flying.

And maybe book proposals, too, he thought.

# 5

NICOLE FOLLOWED ANTHONY inside the room he'd just rented at the disreputable-looking No Tell Motel. The fog had grounded all flights out of D-FW for the night. And the weather wasn't predicted to clear until late tomorrow. To make a bad situation even worse, a computer convention had every hotel in the city fully booked. They'd been lucky to find the lone room they were to share.

Rafe was really going to howl when he heard about it. Maybe she wouldn't tell him about this, either.

She knew how it looked for her and Anthony to check in to the No Tell Motel without a piece of luggage between them. At least they were in a strange town, where no one who knew them was likely to see them.

Behind her, Anthony closed the door with a kick of his boot and tossed the room key on the bed.

"Pretty romantic place, huh?" he said with a raised eyebrow.

Nicole didn't answer.

Sitting down on the bed, Anthony upended the paper sack from the convenience store. A couple of toothbrushes, a tube of toothpaste, a comb and a bottle of nail polish he'd insisted on buying for her scattered on the bed.

Nicole then watched, wide-eyed, as he began breathing into the paper bag.

"What on earth are you doing?" she asked, dumbfounded.

He lowered the sack. "You'd hyperventilate, too, if you were a man and had to live up to this room. Look at it, for heaven's sake."

Nicole looked around the room.

Every wall that wasn't covered in flocked red wallpaper was covered in gold-veined smoked-glass mirror, including the ceiling. The rug on the floor was cheap red plush. But the very worst decorating disaster was the bed. It was round and topped with a black satin spread.

Nicole didn't even want to think about the sheets.

"Or maybe this makes you feel passionate...." He looked up at her.

"The only thing I feel passionate about at the moment is getting some sleep."

"Sleep. You do realize you're shooting my reputation as a legendary lover all to hell...."

"Oh, yes, let's not forget about that reputation you seem to be so fond of."

Anthony brought his hand to his chest. "Oh, *I* don't kiss and tell, mind you." He grinned big time. "But the ladies, bless 'em . . . You do know how they love to talk."

Nicole mumbled something derogatory under her breath as she went to the bed and pulled back the black satin cover. The sheets, incongruously, were white cotton and starchily clean.

"Tell you what, Anthony. I'm going to make you an offer you can't refuse."

"I was hoping you might." His grin was lethal.

"Calm down, Romeo, or you'll be breathing into that paper sack again. Here's the deal. We stay the night here, because we have no choice. But you don't try to live up to the room's decor. As a matter of fact, you don't try anything."

"You're a real spoilsport, you know that?"

"Actually, I think I'm being a pretty good sport," Nicole said, going to take a shower.

Ten minutes later, when she traded places with Anthony, she searched her mind for something to do. Something that would take enough time for Anthony to fall asleep, in case he had any leftover sexy ideas.

Her nails. That was it. She'd add another coat of polish.

She was sitting on the bed in the clothes she'd worn to the concert, wondering if she should just sleep in her T-shirt and underwear, when Anthony came sauntering out of the bathroom with a towel wrapped casually around his waist and his toothbrush stuck in his waistband. His hands were rubbing the sides of his ribs as he stretched lazily.

Nicole watched the towel slip lower on his hips, and gulped.

She tried not to stare. Unsuccessfully.

In need of distraction, she flipped on the TV.

Going back to the bed, she busied herself with her nail polish.

When the picture came on the TV Anthony started to laugh.

She looked up, expecting the Three Stooges.

And then she realized just what sort of movie was on the screen.

*Good grief!*

She should have realized what kinds of films would come with this room. She jumped up and switched off the TV.

Anthony laughed even harder.

"What's so funny!" she demanded, embarrassed, annoyed—and, okay, somewhat aroused.

"You didn't exactly react the way I would have expected you to."

"What did you expect?"

"I don't know." He shrugged. "Maybe that you'd get some ideas you'd want to try out on me. I wouldn't have minded, you know," he said, his eyes dancing. "I'm an accommodating sort of guy."

"I'll just bet."

"After all, we never did get around to discussing your fantasies when you were on my show...."

"This isn't—that wasn't—it."

"Really? What is? You did deliberately sidetrack me to keep me from finding out when you were on the show."

She blushed.

"You're nothing like Dr. Ruth, are you? I didn't think sex therapists were shy when it came to discussing their subject. And you weren't shy when you were on my show. In fact, I had the darndest feeling you were trying to make me blush. What was that all about, anyway?"

Did he know the truth? Nicole wondered uneasily. Was this a setup? No, it couldn't be. Anthony Gawain could do a lot of things, but fogging in a whole city wasn't one of them. That would take a magician of Merlin's caliber.

Maybe it was time she told him about her charade.

She looked around the room, then back at him, and lost her nerve. This wasn't the right place or the right time.

"I'm going to sleep," she announced, setting aside the nail polish and blowing on her painted nails.

"Don't I at least get a good-night kiss?"

"No, you'll ruin my manicure," she said, waving him away.

"Chicken," he accused with a laugh.

HE KNEW HER INSTANT soft snores were as fake as his father's campaign promises.

"Okay, then, I'll tell you one of my fantasies," he offered, way too generously, his voice dripping mannered charm.

She didn't respond.

"Are you listening?"

Still no response, though he was certain she was still awake.

He began.

"This is one of my favorites. I like to call it Tea and Strumpet."

"Tea and Strumpet?" Nicole repeated. "What? You have so many fantasies you have them titled and cataloged in your mind."

"Sure. Don't you?" he asked.

"No."

"Liar," he said teasingly. "I might buy that if you weren't a sex therapist, but anyone interested enough in the subject to make it a career..."

She pretended to snore lightly again.

Anthony plunged on, undeterred by her pretense of disinterest and bent on annoying her.

"I'm doing a show on a festival in a small historic town. I have a reservation for an overnight stay at a bed-and-breakfast to use as a sidebar to the main segment of the show. When I arrive at the bed-and-breakfast, I'm exhausted, because of the long drive, so my hostess shows me to the parlor.

"There she lights a fire and brings me slippers. She leaves and returns a few minutes later with tea and honey cake. While I sip my tea, the hostess performs several tasks for me."

He glanced over at her. Still the pretense of sleep.

"Aren't you going to ask me what tasks? She's really working up a sweat... really getting into what she's doing."

No response.

"What? None of your detailed questions for me, Nikki? Suppose I tell you anyway. First, she gathers all the things she'll need, things like a feather duster, some warm, soapy water, and a plug-in—"

"That's okay, really," Nicole said, interrupting him. "You don't have to tell me, if it's too personal," she said, nearly choking.

"But I want to tell you. I'm enjoying this. Aren't you?"

He couldn't distinguish the noise she made.

"I know it's kinda kinky," he began again, "but I just enjoy the idea of watching a woman dust, vacuum and wash windows while I'm having a spot of tea."

She threw a pillow at him. "Go to sleep," she said to the sound of his pleased-with-himself laughter.

"Sleep . . . That's another of your quaint little euphemisms, right?" he asked hopefully.

"Nope."

When he realized a short while later that the soft snores coming from her side of the bed were genuine, he wondered why he hadn't brought up the book contract. He'd had the perfect opportunity to tell her about it.

He told himself it was because it wasn't the time or the place, all the while knowing that wasn't the real reason.

The real reason was that he didn't want to ask her until he was absolutely certain she'd say yes.

THE FOLLOWING MORNING, Nicole felt as if the sandman had dumped an entire beach in her eyes.

"You're not a morning person, are you?" Anthony commented as she swore at a broken fingernail.

"No shit, Sherlock." Nicole forced herself to put on her cowboy boots and get ready to go to the airport. Anthony's call had confirmed that the planes were flying once again. In a few hours they would be back in L.A., and no one would know about last night.

Nothing had happened. She hadn't wanted anything to happen.

So why did she feel so disappointed?

"Did you have sweet dreams?" Anthony asked, running his fingers through his hair to comb it.

"Umm . . ." Nicole mumbled. She'd dreamed she'd been applying for a job as his political assistant, that he'd been running for office. In the dream she'd performed a private striptease for him on a conference-room table, stripping down to nothing but a string of pearls.

She'd gotten his attention, and the job.

So much for dreams being politically correct.

"It's time," Anthony said, glancing at his watch.

He was right. It was time for them to go, and past time for her to tell him the truth—to tell him she wasn't who he thought she was.

She'd tell him on the drive to the airport.

WHEN ANTHONY OPENED the motel-room door, they were met by a swarm of reporters and photographers. Microphones were shoved in Anthony's face.

Nicole blinked at the bright sunlight as a tall, angular reporter jostling for position yelled out, "Mr. Gawain, do you have any comment on the scandal?"

Scandal?

What scandal? Were they talking about them? Nicole wondered.

Was she going to be part of some tabloid headline?

Oh, no! Her sisters would be horrified, shocked....

And her mother—well, her mother was useless as a role model. She would be delighted that her daughter had finally had an adventure.

Her racing thoughts were stopped by the realization that all the cameras aimed at them were clicking away. She was being recorded on film coming out of a motel room with L.A.'s hottest hunk. She—quiet, shy, retiring Nicole Hart.

She smiled for the cameras.

And then it dawned on her.

Scandal? While being met coming out of the No Tell Motel wasn't the classiest of situations, it was hardly a scandal in this day and age.

Both of them were single. Gawain *was* single, wasn't he? Of course he was, she assured herself. But then, what on earth were the reporters talking about? she wondered, as Anthony held her tightly to his side.

"I don't know what scandal you're talking about," she heard him say, moving them through the throng of reporters and photographers, who weren't giving up easily.

"It's about your cousin—the senator," a blond woman reporter informed him.

Anthony swore beneath his breath.

Nicole could understand why. Whenever a Gawain did something, it always made the news—good or bad. Scandal meant bad.

"I haven't heard anything about it, so I don't have a comment," he said as he and Nicole reached the limo he'd called for to take them to the airport.

A young reporter winked. "Yeah, guess you were kinda busy yourself."

"Your cousin is being sued for paternity by a journalist," another reporter was only too happy to inform him as Anthony glared at the winking reporter.

"It can't be true, then, can it?" Anthony said, while Nicole looked on, watching him try to scotch the rumor with an affable smile. "After all, that would be fraternizing with the enemy, now wouldn't it?" With that, he ducked into the limo with her, and they sped off to catch their plane back to L.A.

So much for no one ever knowing about their little visit to the No Tell Motel . . . And so much for her telling him she wasn't a sex therapist . . .

ANTHONY RAN ALONG the beach outside his Malibu home. His stride was a gentle lope that tossed his dark hair from side to side. He could just make out the Channel Islands on the horizon in the pinky-mauve dusk as he worked off the fish and chips he'd eaten at the beach shack.

At the same time, he was trying to get the trip to Dallas out of his mind. His date with Nicole Hart hadn't exactly been a fiasco, but it had come pretty close. He smiled as he thought about it, the sand warm against his bare feet, its pull flexing the muscles of his thighs. A red-tailed hawk sailed by on an updraft, catching his attention briefly before he went back to recalling how last night had been sort of fun, in a goofy kind of way. It just hadn't gone as planned. And he always hated that.

He had grown up being groomed to be a politician, like all the men in his family. It was part of his heritage. While it was a comfortable life, it was also a life in which everything was planned for him. His very existence had been mapped out for him, from where he would go to school to who his friends would be. And he'd gone along with it all, willingly, believing everything he was spoonfed, because he wanted to be a good son.

Until he found out that everything he believed was a lie. Found out his mother had been pregnant with another man's son when she married the man he'd thought was his father. From the day he'd overheard the truth from his mother's lips, when he learned that his real father wasn't her husband, he'd become a rebel.

He couldn't tell his father he wasn't his son, but he couldn't pretend that he was, either. His political "heritage" was nothing but a lie. So he tried to be as different as possible from what his father expected of his son.

He dressed in black leather, was thrown out of the best prep schools, and courted unacceptable friends. Eventually his father washed his hands of him. He transferred the expectations he'd had for him to his willing younger brother.

Restless and unfocused, Anthony had always enjoyed being the black sheep of the family. But lately that role had grown pale. It didn't provide the same satisfaction it once had. He'd become bored with being a rebel. Maybe it was time for him to stand *for* something instead of *against* everything.

The chance to be published might give him a podium.

Nicole Hart was the only stumbling block. He had a feeling it was going to take some pretty fancy footwork to get her to agree to see him again. And he was going to have to see her again if he wanted to write the book. His agent had made it clear the publisher wanted both of them under contract for the book.

But that wasn't the sole reason he wanted to see Nicole Hart again. On their date he'd glimpsed a shyer side of the sexy sex therapist—a side that intrigued him.

# 6

*Los Angeles Times*

Entertainment News:

ITEM . . . If the photograph accompanying this
column is any indication, it appears Mr. Gawain
and Ms. Hart are an item. But what this columnist wants to know is whether Mr. Gawain is
courting the sexy sex therapist for professional
or private reasons.... Guess we'll all have to stay
tuned to "The Anthony Gawain Show" to find
out.

"I TAKE IT MS. HART said yes," Mark Bates observed
in a smarmy tone, studying the photograph of Anthony and Nicole accompanying the Entertainment
News column. Their regular breakfast meeting at
Patrick's Roadhouse was their first meeting since Anthony had taken Nicole to the concert in Dallas.

Anthony looked up from the black-and-white tile
floor he'd been gazing at, lost in thought. "What are
you talking about?"

Pointing to the photograph, Mark handed him the newspaper. The photograph had been taken in Dallas.

"I didn't get around to asking Ms. Hart about the book contract," Anthony said, skimming the column. He raised his eyebrow at the columnist's jab about his possibly seeing the sex therapist for professional reasons. There were many ways her comment could be construed, and he was sure the columnist knew it.

The Gawain family certainly had their hands full, what with both his implied impotence and his cousin's alleged fertility in the news. He could just see the meetings going on behind closed doors at the Gawain family compound as they tried to put the best spin possible on the publicity. Trouble was, he had such a bad reputation, nothing could worsen it, and there wasn't much good to be found in a journalist suing a senator—a very married senator—for paternity.

"Ms. Hart?" Mark repeated with a smirk in his voice. "You spend a night at the No Tell Motel with her, and you're still calling her Ms. Hart? Boy, those blue-blooded manners of yours really kick in sometimes, don't they? What do you mean, you didn't ask her about the book contract? You had all night. What did you do at the No Tell Motel, anyway? You don't have to take the name literally, you know...." Finish-

ing a bite of his omelet, he added, "Details. I want details."

Anthony took a sip of his hot coffee, ignoring the
juvenile remarks. "We talked," he answered, tipping
his chair back on two legs.

"Talked?"

Anthony nodded.

"Then I had a much better evening than you, and I
didn't even have a date," Mark boasted. "I went to this
new place called Miss Olivia's Finishing School. It's a
real classy strip club, with a white-gloved doorman
and everything." Without waiting for Anthony to
show interest, he continued. "There was even a con-
ference room with a fax, it was so upscale. And I hear
the girls pull in such big tips that they have portfolios
bigger than their monied patrons."

"What did you say the name of the place was?"
Anthony asked, settling his chair back down as a
show tune played on the jukebox in the background.

"I'll take you there if you like," Mark offered. "It's
called Miss Olivia's Finishing School, and every night
the young ladies are *real polite* at their 'coming-out'
party. You'd swear you were at an exclusive all-girls
school. It's safe sex, because there isn't any. Everyone
is well behaved, and the girls are untouchable."

"Sounds interesting," Anthony mused, his long
forefinger rubbing his chin.

Mark's face registered surprise at Anthony's comment. The two of them never socialized together. "You want to go with me one night, then?"

"No. I meant it was interesting in terms of a topic for one of my shows."

"Really?"

Anthony nodded. "I'd like to explore what a place like Miss Olivia's Finishing School says about sex and our culture in the nineties. These upscale gathering places where men go to feed their erotic fantasies are springing up all over the country. I noticed there was one in Dallas called the Cabaret Royale—housed in a mansion."

"Well, if you're really thinking about doing a show, I could do some background stuff for you. You know, interview some of the girls . . ."

Anthony didn't comment right away on Mark's eager offer to help. After finishing his coffee, he said, "I would really like to hear what women think about these places . . . to find out if they frequent them with dates."

"We could even do a companion show the next sweeps period titled 'What Do Men Want'?" Mark volunteered.

"Put that down to explore. I think it's a good idea," Anthony agreed.

"Everything here okay?" their young waitress asked, placing their check facedown on the newspaper after ascertaining that it was. She then moved on to help another waitress.

Mark glanced down at the newspaper beneath the check. He studied the picture of Anthony snapped by the photographer in Dallas when the paternity scandal involving his cousin broke—the scandal that had disappeared from the news when the woman suddenly withdrew her suit for some unknown reason. In the photograph, Anthony had Nicole in tow rather possessively.

"So when are you planning on asking Ms. Hart to write the book with you?" he asked. "Your agent keeps bugging me to get you moving on it."

"I'm going to ask her. It's just that the timing hasn't been right so far, that's all. It's important that she see the project in a favorable light. If you recall, she gave me a pretty tough time on the show. I don't think it would be easy to persuade her to do it, if she got turned off the idea for some reason."

"I should think anyone would jump at the chance to cowrite a book," Mark disagreed, clearly misunderstanding Anthony's argument.

"It isn't the writing the book I think she'd object to," he explained. "It's having me as the cowriter. In case you didn't notice when she was on the show, she gave the distinct impression that I annoyed her somehow. I want her to get to know me a little better, so that she thinks the idea of the two of us writing a book together about relationships is a good idea."

"Then you plan to date her a couple of times before you actually broach the subject of writing the book...."

"Not date her, exactly," Anthony hedged. "Just sort of see her." Not feeling entirely comfortable with his plan, he picked up the check and the newspaper. He nevertheless dismissed the disquiet he felt, saying goodbye to Mark and paying the check on the way out. He paid with cash. Most celebrities paid with plastic, but he was too impatient. And patience, he knew, was what it was going to take to get Nicole Hart to see things his way.

Pulling out of the parking lot, he considered what sort of "non-date" to invite Nicole on.

He had an invitation to a party at the twelve-acre Beverly Hills estate of record mogul David Geffen, which had once been the home of movie mogul Jack Warner. That would impress the socks off most anyone. And then he remembered Nicole's bare feet in sandals when she'd been on his show. And rubbing her bare feet at the No Tell Motel. She had great feet.

No, trying to impress her wasn't the way to go, he decided.

He could suggest they meet at the Rendezvous Court of the Biltmore and go to the Museum of Contemporary Art. Naw. That idea was a bit too pretentious, he decided, discarding it.

A blonde in a British racing green XJS Jag convertible honked and waved as she rode by. He would never get used to people acting as if they knew him just because he was a celebrity. Distracted, he returned her wave in an offhand way.

As he reached to turn on the radio, his gaze fell on the newspaper lying open on the seat of the Jeep. He had the answer to his search for a date that would work in his favor. The newspaper carried an ad for an appearance by the hot young comedian Jerry Seinfeld at the Celebrity Theater. The comedian's sitcom dealt with modern relationships and had a cult following. It would get the two of them talking about the subject matter of the book.

Picking up the car phone, he placed a call as he maneuvered through traffic and secured two tickets to the show. Punching in his office number, he got Nicole's number from a staff member on his show.

NICOLE SAT ON THE SOFA with her notebook in hand, her pen tapping an empty page. A few minutes later, she sprawled out, legs hanging over the sofa arm. Moments later, she was peering into the yawning refrigerator, trying to decide if she was really hungry.

Slamming the door, she took herself in hand and went back to the sofa and the empty page.

Her screenplay wasn't going well.

"Cat and Spouse" still wasn't coming together like she wanted it to. Maybe it was because she was tired. She'd spent the day working as a movie extra, playing a woman crossing the street.

Her hand reached for the remote control of the television. She put it back down. No, she was looking for a distraction, when she knew the only way to make the scene work was to make herself work.

The phone rang.

She pounced on it. After all, she couldn't be responsible for it distracting her, she told her conscience.

"Anthony?" she said, with surprise in her voice.

"I feel badly about how the evening went . . ." she heard him saying. Why was he feeling badly? she wondered. She had thought the evening had gone a little too well. In fact, if she was honest with herself, the real reason she was having trouble writing was that she was busy hoping that he both would and wouldn't call her.

"I could pick you up from your office, if you'd like . . ." he was saying.

Her office! Oh, no, he couldn't! She didn't have one. She wasn't a practicing sex therapist. She wasn't a sex therapist at all.

"Nicole? Are you there?"

"Yes. Yes, I'm here," she answered.

"Well, what do you think?" he asked.

"I, ah..." She hadn't heard much of what he'd been saying to her.

"If you don't like Seinfeld, we could do something else. I just thought his show would be fun."

"Seinfeld. Yes, I do like him."

"Then you'll go?"

She shouldn't. But she wanted to. Actually, she *should* go. She needed to explain about not being a sex therapist. She'd let that lie go on far too long.

"Nicole?"

"I'd love to go," she said, squinching her eyes closed. Telling him her home address before she could lose her nerve, she hung up the phone, feeling both a rush of excitement and a wave of nausea.

What had she done?

She couldn't even blame Rafe for this one.

But this wasn't really a date. It was strictly so that she could tell him the truth. To get rid of the guilt she felt over the huge amount of money he'd spent flying her to Dallas for the Garth Brooks concert.

Why had he done that?

She still wasn't clear about what exactly was going on between the two of them. There was a certain combative chemistry, a chemistry that was sexual in nature, humming between the two of them, but . . . Oh, how had she gotten herself into this mess?

Her life was beginning to resemble her screenplay!

She stared down at the blank page again.

The thoughts that came weren't any she could write down. They were about black satin, hard abs and sinewy thighs. About sleek black hair cascading to hide a masculine face in the throes of passion as Anthony braced himself above her on strong arms.

How had spending an innocent night with Anthony Gawain turned her into the equivalent of a lust-crazed teenager? Throwing down her notebook and pen in disgust, she went in search of a bag of M & M's. Somewhere she'd read that chocolate was a remedy for frustration.

"WHAT ARE YOU THINKING about?" Anthony asked. Pulling her to him, he lifted her chin with his forefinger, tipping her face up to his in the moonlight.

The Seinfeld show had been wonderful fun. They had both howled along with the audience at Seinfeld's take on the differences between men and women. Dinner afterward had been simple and fitting—a trip to the In-N-Out for cheeseburgers.

After that, when Anthony had suggested she come back to his place in Malibu and go for a walk with him on the beach, she'd thought it was a good idea; she'd burn off the calories and work up her courage to tell him the truth.

Only it hadn't worked out that way.

Anthony had pushed up the sleeves of his white linen suit jacket and rolled up the legs of his matching suit pants. Loosening his tie, he'd coaxed her to shed her pumps and stroll barefoot with him in the surf.

The breeze off the ocean whipping the damp hem of her long, cream-colored chiffon skirt also teased at their hair. She was reminded of her erotic fantasy of Anthony making love to her. The salty sea breeze only fed the magic as the surf lapped at their feet.

"I was, um...thinking about the trip to Texas," she answered.

"Yes, that was a bit of a disaster. I do hope you've forgiven me for it."

"The fog ... It ... it couldn't be helped," she stammered. She was having trouble forming sentences, and feeling she was faint and giddy. Anthony was wild and gorgeous, silhouetted in the moonlight. His touch burned her skin, and streamers of desire raced in a game of sensual tag from his body to hers. A mental image flashed in her mind of the famous movie scene of a couple, their bodies entwined in an intense embrace, rolling over and over in the surf and sand.

"I promise you that despite my reputation—" he brushed a skimming kiss over her lips "—I don't make it a habit to drag a woman off to a motel on a first date and then have a photographer record it and put it in the newspaper the following morning like a notch on a bedpost."

"Oh? How many dates do you usually wait?" Nicole asked, fighting madly for control.

"I don't have any hard-and-fast rules," he answered, his lips grazing her ear. "It depends on the woman."

He rubbed her chin with the pad of his thumb. "Can I ask you a question?"

She nodded.

"Do you have any hard-and-fast rules about kissing on the second date?"

"It depends on the man," she instantly replied.

"He feels like it would be a good idea," Anthony said, lowering his lips to hers.

Still primed from her erotic fantasy of him, she felt her mouth open at the touch of his lips on hers. His tongue probed past her teeth to plunder, to take. Her passion escalated, ready to spiral out of control. He slid his hands into her hair, tilting her head while his kiss deepened, rocking her to the tips of her bare toes. In fact, he had them curling in the sand.

Anthony Gawain was no sensible woman's idea of Prince Charming. His was the dark, dangerous allure of a man who would conquer and then leave. He was everything she'd sworn she would never fall for.

With her last ounce of reason, Nicole broke free of his powerful spell, pulling away. "This isn't such a good idea. I don't know you. Not really."

Anthony took her hand, kissing her palm. "I have an idea how to fix that."

Nicole's laugh was shaky. "I'll just bet."

"I'm serious.... I want to ask you for your help. I'm planning on writing a book."

"A book?" She hadn't been prepared for that. "What kind of book?" she asked suspiciously, pulling her hand away.

"A book based on my sweeps-week show exploring what women want."

"Oh."

"I thought, with you being a sex therapist and all..." He dropped a kiss on her nose.

Now was the time to tell him the truth.

But then it dawned on her. He hadn't been *dating* her. All he wanted was a sex therapist to help him with research for his book idea. Instead of coming right out with the request, he'd been devious, dishonest. He'd asked her out on the pretense of a date to soften her up for his cause. A handsome, charismatic charmer, running true to form. And she'd fallen for it. Only moments ago, she'd been putty in his hands.

No, she wasn't going to tell him the truth. She'd continue to let him think she was a sex therapist for a while longer. It served him right.

It was her turn to string *him* along.

"I think it's time you took me home," she said, starting to walk ahead of him on the beach. The romance had gone out of the evening, though moonlight still shimmered off the water and the sea still ebbed and flowed with a curling splash of foam.

He caught up to her with a couple of his long-legged strides.

"Nicole, wait," he said, catching her hand in his. "I take it, then, that you don't want to help me with the book...."

"No, I'll help you," she heard herself saying. She hoped it was a satisfying revenge she was hungry for, and not more of Anthony's Gawain's sweet kisses— that drugged her senses.

And she hoped the person she was telling the biggest lie to wasn't herself.

RAFE BROUGHT HER MAIL in with him when he stopped by the following morning to ask her opinion about a design he was working on for a community theater project.

"Anything interesting?" he asked, flopping down on her sofa, his hand reaching for the remote control of the TV.

Nicole flipped through her mail, cataloging it out loud. "A bill from Nordstrom, a writers' newsletter, and a postcard from my mother." She laid the bill and the newsletter on the mantel and scanned the postcard. "Mother's cowboy took first place in bronc busting."

"How's your shower?" Rafe asked, flipping on the TV to his favorite soap opera—"The Bold and the Beautiful," which was set in the world of fashion.

"Fine. You get my vote for first place in plumbing. It hasn't leaked since you fixed it," she said, joining him on the sofa to watch along.

"Who do you think Brooke is pregnant by, Eric or Ridge?" Rafe asked about the characters on the screen.

With his dark good looks, Ridge Forrester looked too much like Anthony Gawain for Nicole's comfort. She identified with Brooke, who had been used by the handsome Ridge. "I think she's pregnant by Eric," she answered, coming out of her musings.

"Looks to me like she's going to be spending a lot of time working with Ridge in Paris now that she's developed that new fabric," Rafe said. "Working together is bound to start making things complicated between them."

Working together. That was what she and Anthony were going to be doing. He'd asked for her help researching his book idea, and she'd agreed to meet him on Sunday. They were going to have a picnic on the beach and talk about the way he planned to do the book. Was she crazy?

A commercial break had Rafe turning to her to ask, "So I haven't seen you since you went to Texas with Gawain. Give."

"How did you know—?" Her eyes narrowed with suspicion. "Or did you know the concert was in Texas all along, and neglected to tell me?"

"I didn't know."

Nicole made neck-strangling motions with her hands.

"Honest. I didn't know until I saw your picture in the Entertainment News column, when the two of you were coming out of the—"

"Don't remind me," Nicole groaned, picking up Rafe's portfolio of designs for the show he was costuming.

"What design is giving you trouble?" she asked, looking through them.

"This one," he said, picking it out. "What do you think about the proportion?"

Nicole studied it for a few moments. "I like it. Why? What did you think was wrong with it?"

"Nothing. It's only that the actress it's for is a first-class— Well, she's difficult."

"Trust me, the costume is lovely," Nicole said, putting the sketch back with the others. The soap opera came back on, and they sat watching the final fifteen minutes of it in silence.

When it was over, Rafe switched off the TV. He turned to her, grabbing her hands. "Okay, now for the really juicy details. Did you and Gawain do it in Dallas?"

"Rafe!"

"Well, did you?" Rafe loved to gossip. Even about himself. Maybe especially about himself, Nicole thought with a smile. He'd told her things about himself that made *her* flush, and told them without so much as batting an eye.

"No, we didn't *do* it," Nicole said firmly, pulling her hands away.

"Yeah, right." Rafe stared at her with an expression of feigned belief.

"We didn't," she insisted. "Anthony is just a— He's a friend."

"Sure, he is. You're trying to tell me the guy spent mucho bucks flying you to Texas for a sold-out concert, rented a limo, et cetera, and you think of him as just a friend. He must be somewhere now slitting his wrists."

"Rafe, be real. I'm not his type."

"You're telling me Gawain didn't get naked, then?"

"The best I can give you is seminaked."

"Now we're getting somewhere."

"No, we aren't. *I* didn't get seminaked. We *slept* together, but nothing happened. We were two strangers, sharing a room because we were fogged in. That's all."

"If you say so," Rafe said in a humoring tone. "So when are you going to see Anthony again?"

"Sunday."

"What does he have planned? A trip on a yacht, a balloon ride . . ."

"Nothing like that. Just something simple. We're having a picnic at the beach."

"Real unromantic, that," Rafe said drolly.

"Ra-afe!"

"What?" he asked, all innocence.

"Shut up."

"My aren't we touchy about our innocent friendship!"

"It *is* innocent. Anthony's planning to write a book, and I promised to help him, nothing more."

"So he knows you're a screenwriter, then?"

Nicole shook her head.

"No?"

"The book is a follow-up to the show I was on—about women and what they want. He needs me to help him with the research."

"So you're still pretending to be a sex therapist?" Rafe asked, a wide grin on his face.

"Something like that."

"You're a bad woman. Really bad," he said with gleeful respect.

Nicole shook her head. She knew she was in real trouble when she had Rafe's respect.

## 7

THE WEATHER COOPERATED with their oceanside picnic, the morning fog rolling out to be replaced by warm sunshine and a gentle breeze. On the sandy beach below his contemporary cement-block home, Anthony and Nicole shared a wholesome take-out lunch from John's Garden restaurant with the shore birds, laughing at their antics.

Pulling a chilled bottle of champagne from a bucket of ice—a child's sand pail with a mermaid on it—Anthony poured them each a paper cupful. Lifting his cup to hers, he made a toast.

"To our successful collaboration, Nikki. Shall we get down to it?"

The way he said it made it sound more like a lascivious proposition than a call to work. Maybe it was just the way he looked, with his dark hair blowing free in the wind like a stallion's mane.

He looked completely relaxed in a pair of comfortable old jeans and an oversize black polo shirt. She smiled at his footwear. Only a self-confident rebel would have the nerve to wear the T-strap sandals he had on—sockless, of course.

The stylish Oliver Peoples eyeglasses he pulled out of his pocket didn't diminish his masculine appeal. They only lent him an air of intellectual mystery.

She was in way over her head, all right.

And she wasn't even in the water.

He took out a small notebook and flipped it open on the blanket where they'd eaten their picnic lunch.

"What's that?" Nicole asked, trying to read the page upside down.

"I've made some notes for the book. I thought you could give me your professional take on my ideas."

Nicole nodded. Her professional "take." She took a sip of champagne. Banishing any guilt over her charade she said, "Shoot." After all, Anthony deserved to be deceived, because he'd done just that to her. He'd asked her out under false pretenses, when he'd really wanted her help, not her body.

Looking down at his list, Anthony proceeded.

"Okay, would you agree that women of the nineties find predictable men boring? And that woman really want a man they can't be sure of?"

"Women of the nineties?" Nicole repeated. "I hope not. Sure, it's always been true that those men have appeal. But I don't think that kind of man has necessarily ever been a woman's conscious choice.

Women have been conditioned to accept being the spoils of victory. Conditioned, I might add, by men who couldn't be depended on. I'm rather confident that women of the nineties will break free of the old cultural baggage."

"You want to run that by me in English?" Anthony said, tossing back the rest of his champagne, finishing it in one swallow.

Nicole searched in her mind for a way to encapsulate her personal beliefs. "Okay. A smart woman of today knows that real men are men who can be counted on, not men who leave at the slightest provocation, abandoning their responsibilities by using the bogus claim, 'male prerogative,' which won't play in today's world."

"Simple English?" Anthony asked hopefully.

Nicole knew she was floundering; she had never been able to express her anger, frustration and pain over her own father's leaving—over the damage it had done, and continued to do, to her self-esteem. Taking a deep breath, she said, "Real men don't say 'I do' when they mean 'I don't.'"

"O-kay," Anthony said, quickly looking down at his notes and then moving on. "What do you think about men with sexual power?"

"I'm not sure I know exactly what you mean," she answered, reminding herself that a sex therapist

wouldn't blush at the question, even if it had been
asked by a man with sexual power to burn.

Anthony crumpled his paper cup and made a playful hook shot into the basket beside them on the blanket. Looking at her, he explained. "You know—men
with intelligence, creativity, or some attribute that
gives them sexual power when it comes to women,
even though they may not be particularly attractive
physically."

Like a gamboling goat, he'd blundered unawares
onto her hot button.

It infuriated Nicole that society found it perfectly
acceptable for men to judge women solely on their
looks, while a woman was expected to judge men on
a variety of attributes.

A woman could be found sexy only if she had traditional prettiness and curves in all the right places.
Men, however, could be skinny, or pot-bellied, could
range from obnoxious to cruel, and still be considered sexy if they had money, power or talent. With all
three, a man was a god. Just ask one of them.

"Are women allowed to have sexual power if they
aren't deemed attractive? I don't think so. Perhaps
what you have there is an old husbands' tale, better
known as wishful thinking on the part of the male."

"Really?" Anthony questioned. He leaned back on his elbows. "So then how do you explain a beautiful woman with an unattractive man?"

Nicole riffled her memory for anything she'd read for a comeback. Maybe something she'd picked up in her research for her appearance on Anthony's show. Finally she recalled something she could use.

"Simple. A woman who is unsure of herself, for whatever reason, might choose someone she felt secure with. She might feel an unattractive man would be blinded by her beauty and fail to see her insecurities."

"Whew, you're tough."

"What else have you got there?" Nicole asked. It felt good to discuss her feelings with a man while maintaining a degree of anonymity.

"Not football," Anthony said, going for levity. "Even I'm evolved enough to know that football is not what women want—or even like."

"That's because football is the sport of testosterone. That's why it's played in the early fall, when men's testosterone is at its annual high." She couldn't recall where on earth she'd gleaned that odd bit of information, but it did sound impressive.

Anthony flipped his notebook closed.

"So much for my notes."

"What do you mean?"

"Come on, Nikki. We both know this isn't going anywhere. Why don't you give me a break and help me get some sort of handle on the book? I'm open to any ideas you might have. It's not like you haven't noticed I'm striking out."

"Why do you want to write about the subject?"

"Because of the response the show we did got. The ratings were phenomenal. It got a publisher's interest, and I think it's an important question a lot of people would like answered."

Nicole thought for a moment, rubbing her hands on her white cotton slacks. When she finally spoke, she didn't try to sound like an expert; her words came from her heart.

"I think women are tired of not being loved."

"What do you mean?" Anthony asked, giving her his full attention.

"I mean *loved*, in the fullest sense of the word. I mean having their emotional needs met, as well as their physical ones. What it really translates into is, women want respect. They want their wishes treated with respect."

Gaining momentum, she went on. "They don't want to be humored. They don't want to be condescended to. They don't want to be ignored, even benignly. And they don't want to be lied to. They want a man who is faithful, not a man who is 'sort of' faithful."

"And you think women aren't getting what they want—that men are clueless," Anthony said, hearing the bitterness in her voice.

"Exactly. Women are tired of the old rhetoric. Tired of being told they must be ladies—that is, submissive, polite and accepting—so that men will love them.

"That's like the advice they used to give in women's magazines, advising single women to let their dates win at tennis or whatever. It's insulting to both the woman and the man.

"Don't you think it's patently ridiculous that women are afraid to frighten big strong men with their—gasp—needs?"

Anthony chuckled at the head of steam she'd built up as she talked. "Why don't you say what you really mean?" he asked her teasingly.

"I'm serious, Anthony. If you want to write a book about what women really want, you have to consider that women are simply not getting enough of their needs met. While it's true that women enjoy nurturing others, they need to be nurtured as well.

"The question isn't so much what women want, but rather why women are afraid to ask for what they want. Afraid of identifying their own needs and then asking—no, demanding—that their needs be met. Afraid that being a strong woman will drive a man away."

"Well, you can't say I'm not listening and learning," Anthony told her, reaching back into the basket behind him. "As I recall, one of your needs is chocolate." His eyes dancing, he handed her a white box tied with gold ribbon.

"What's this?"

"Heminger's fudge. It's made the old-fashioned way. They mix it in copper kettles and prepare it on a marble table."

"Looks like a bribe to me," she said, nonetheless slipping the gold ribbon from the box to open it. The sweet aroma of chocolate greeted her when she opened the lid and lifted the tissue.

"It is a bribe."

"And has this worked for you before?" she asked. "Champagne and chocolate?" She bit into a piece of the rich chocolate fudge she'd selected. It had the creamiest consistency of any chocolate she'd ever tasted.

Anthony shrugged. "I've never made this kind of proposition to a woman before," he assured her with his easy grace. Lifting her finger to his lips, he licked a speck of chocolate from it ever so slowly. His tongue felt warm and exciting on her skin . . . and suggestive.

He looked up into her eyes to gauge her reaction.

Her responding glance was rueful. "Why don't I believe you?"

"I don't know. I thought we were making friends. I thought I'd convinced you I wasn't such a bad guy, and that you at least liked me a little better than you did when you guested on my show. After that particular show I had to check and make sure the family jewels were still attached. Your sharp wit cut pretty close to the bone."

"I think you're up to it," she assured him, not buying his "vulnerable" act. Then she blushed when she realized the pun she'd inadvertently made. He was smiling wickedly.

"Didn't they teach you how not to blush at sex therapists' school?"

"I'm *not* blushing." She ducked her head to cover the fact that of course she was.

He took her hand and pulled her up with him. "Come on. Let's go for a stroll on the beach, and I'll proposition you."

"What an offer," she said, her tone flippant. "I don't think you have to worry, Anthony—you've still got balls." She couldn't believe the gibe had slipped past her lips. When would she learn to censor her quips?

"Ms. Hart!"

"Didn't they teach you how not to blush at talk-show-host school?" she asked, batting his own words back at him.

"Touché, Nikki," he said, flashing her a grin as they began their stroll along the beach.

NICOLE STOPPED TO PICK up a pretty seashell from the beach.

The book forgotten for the moment, Anthony watched her turning the shell over in her hand, studying it.

Somehow he had connected with this intense, sexy, unpredictable woman. A woman so shy she'd slept with her clothes on when they were stranded overnight together in the motel. Yet she'd baited him with sexual innuendo on his talk show. She'd purposely gotten to him.

She wasn't the simple, uncomplicated woman he'd thought he wanted, that was for sure.

What was her agenda? What had she wanted to achieve from being on his show? Some people guested just for the kick they got out of appearing on television. Most guests agreed to appear because they wanted to promote something, wanted the exposure the wide audience of television viewers gave them.

A possible answer to his question surfaced in his mind, a viable reason for her having wanted to be on his show. It was logical and simple.

Maybe Nicole Hart wanted to be a celebrity.

It had been done before, by other therapists. Dr. Ruth was one of the most successful at promoting herself. She'd carried it so far that she had actually appeared as a celebrity model in a designer's fashion show, for heaven's sake.

Nicole had seemed prepared for *him*, had in fact seemed to be gunning for him. Was it because she didn't like him? Or was it his image that pushed her buttons? The columnists' carefully constructed image of him was the one the public knew. Had her baiting him been based on her own personal feelings about him? Or had it all been carefully scripted in her mind? Had her reason all along been the desire to create controversy? To gain media attention?

Or was there some reason she wanted to dupe him?

Had she?

Was she?

Did she even like him? Would she agree to write a book with him? If celebrity was her goal, surely she would.

But what if it wasn't?

He should have told her about the book offer before now. The longer he waited, the worse the situation got.

Though he knew it was time he told her, he couldn't. Not yet.

He'd become interested in her as a woman. Interested as he had never been before. She had somehow managed to make him want to let down his guard, to tell her his secrets, to show her his weaknesses.

He needed to see if she was interested in him as a man, not just as a celebrity.

Nicole slipped the seashell into the pocket of her white shirt and turned to look up at him. "So . . . I'm waiting . . ." she said.

"For what?"

"Your proposition, remember?"

"Right. I want you to help me . . . prepare a survey."

"What kind of survey?" she asked, as a Frisbee disk sailed by with a dog chasing it.

"A survey to find out what women want. To find out what really works in today's relationships. I want you to help me work up a set of questions."

Nicole didn't say yes or no. The dog raced past them with the Frisbee in his mouth, running back to the young boy who'd tossed it.

"How do you plan to conduct your survey?" she asked, as they continued walking down the beach.

"I haven't thought that far," he answered with a shrug. "Why, does it matter?"

"Sure, it matters. The way you conduct your survey could well influence the sort of questions you ask, as well as the success of the survey."

"Really?"

"I think so. People feel freer to answer questions when a survey is done anonymously. You could do it by mail, like some of the magazines do. Or you could hand them out to your studio audience to fill out and mail in.

"If you did it by phone, for instance, a lot of women would probably hang up on you—not to mention the problem of answering machines.

"Or were you planning to date a whole lot of different women and give each one of them your survey personally? That would be a great gimmick. Or is that what this is? Do you really have a publisher's interest? Are you really planning on writing a book?" she asked suspiciously.

"Sure I am."

"Okay, if that's true, then what sort of questions would you ask, since you've given this subject so much thought?"

Thinking for a moment or two, he came up with something she'd brought up when she appeared on his show.

"One thing I'd ask about is sexual chemistry. I'd like to know how important it is to a woman."

"What kind of question is that?"

"Well, for instance, why have women, as you suggested, always made choices with their heads instead of their loins. Do they convince themselves of a man's desirability when he fits all the right slots in the marriageability chart they have in their minds?

"Why aren't women subject to the rule of the loins, like men are? Don't women ever marry a man because he turns them on beyond reason?" Thinking of his mother, he asked, "Are they ever truly honest with themselves, at least?"

"Okay, so you have given it some thought." she agreed. "You've come up with a valid question that bears exploring. Include it in your survey, and I think you might be surprised by the answers you get from women today."

"How about you?" he asked.

"Me?"

"Yes, you. Do you think sexual chemistry is important?" he asked, pulling her into his arms and putting her on the spot.

Nicole swallowed. "Ah...I...ah...I think it's important, sure," she answered.

"What sort of woman are you, Nikki?" he asked, his voice low. "Are you a woman who is always in control, who is ruled by her head?" He slipped his fingers into the pocket of her shirt. When he fished out the seashell she'd stashed there, he could feel the budding of her nipple against the backs of his fingers.

"Are you a pretty package, but empty of life, like this shell?" he asked, holding it up to her. "Or are you a woman full of life—a woman who is at least sometimes ruled by her loins?" He pulled her against him suggestively, invitingly.

"Oh, no, you don't, lover boy," she said, deflecting the sexual chemistry heating up between them once again. Dodging his question, she danced away from his embrace. "I'm helping you with the survey, not taking it," she retorted over her shoulder as she started jogging back down the beach in the direction they'd come.

Catching up to her, he allowed her to avoid his question. Instead, he asked another one. "Why is it that you think women have changed in the nineties and men haven't?"

Nicole laughed, taking a detour to splash in the surf. "The answer to that is simple enough. Men don't change because they will always like comics, the Three Stooges, and instruction manuals. Men don't change because they don't want to—and, more important, because they haven't felt they had to change.

"You know—what with all those stories in the eighties about there being a man shortage. Stories probably started by men. The only way men will

change is if women change them, because men lack
the discipline to change."

"Wouldn't it be better to find a nice guy like me to
start out with?" Anthony said with a wink.

"*You?* A nice guy?" Nicole chortled.

Anthony made a pretense of looking offended by
her doubt. "Sure, I'm a nice guy. I bought you chocolate, didn't I?"

"Not without an ulterior motive, you didn't. You
bought it to get me to agree to help you make up your
survey, remember?" She dropped down onto the
blanket they'd picnicked on.

"Then you agree to help me with the survey?" he
ventured, joining her on the blanket.

Nicole didn't reply. Instead, she rummaged in the
box of fudge, selecting a piece that was chock full of
crunchy walnuts. Popping it into her mouth, she pretended to consider the idea.

He wanted to spank her. He wanted to kiss her. But
if he kissed her he wouldn't be able to hear what she
had to say. And he so enjoyed hearing what she had
to say.

It was refreshing to be with a woman who didn't
hang on his every word and agree with his every
opinion. Being a celebrity isolated one in that way.
People humored you or courted you. They told you
what they thought you wanted to hear.

Her pink tongue slipped out to lick a speck of fudge from the corner of her mouth. He found himself wondering what kind of sounds Nicole made when making love.

She was a woman who knew how to kiss a man. She had a sort of hunger—a really hot mouth, and a wicked tongue. There was a certain reckless abandon to her kisses, making him think she would be a spontaneous lover.

He wanted to spend an entire day in bed with her.

He wanted to linger over lovemaking with her. He wanted to pamper, massage her. And it would be heaven to have a woman you could talk to in bed. He was after a meeting of minds, as well as bodies. He imagined the wanton words she would whisper in his ear.

With a smile, he visualized her on top, in control, so that he could look at her.

"What are you thinking about?"

Nicole's question was like a splash of cold water on his overheated thoughts. "I...ah... I was...thinking about how we might go about...uh...making up the questions for the survey."

"I haven't yet agreed to do it with you," Nicole reminded.

"Oh, you'll do it," he told her, his thoughts more on what he'd been imagining than on the survey.

"What makes you so sure?" she demanded, slipping her bare feet back into her sandals. She waited patiently for his answer, which was slow in coming.

"You'll do it, Nikki, because you're a sex therapist."

"What?"

"The answers to the survey would benefit your practice. A smart woman like you wouldn't turn down the opportunity to broaden her knowledge just because I happen to make you a little nervous."

"You do not make me nervous."

She fiddled with buttoning her shirt over her tank top while he looked at her doubtfully.

"Well, you don't," she insisted.

He leaned in closer to her. "I do when I kiss you, Nikki," he said, his voice a husky whisper. "I make you plenty nervous then, don't I?"

She opened her mouth to deny his words, but he claimed her mouth instead. Taking gentle care, he brushed his lips against hers in a sweet, soft caress.

"Did you like that?" he whispered.

She made a soft sound of pleasure.

He lowered her to the blanket, covering her body with his. He kissed her again, this time hard, deep and long.

His blood throbbed through his veins, and he felt a pulsating need for her.

Then, abruptly, he stopped kissing her and levered himself to one side of her, his breathing heavy.

"What's wrong?" she asked.

"I'm making *myself* nervous."

# 8

"GET REAL, RAFE. You're good, but you're not that good."

"O ye of little faith," Rafe said cockily, sure of his ability to make the shot.

"Come on, Rafe. Even Willie Mosconi would have trouble making that shot."

"So put your money where your mouth is, lady." He seemed not the least bit disturbed by her lack of faith in his skill as he set up the brightly colored balls carefully on the green felt.

"You're on," Nicole agreed, laying a crumpled dollar bill on the rail of the pool table.

The two of them had been in need of a serious dose of fun. It had been Rafe's idea to come to the Hollywood Athletic Club to play on one of their forty-two tables, which rented for twelve bucks an hour.

He'd made the case for going by insisting it was good business for them, as lots of Hollywood stars played pool at the Hollywood Athletic Club. Making their faces familiar was a vital part of networking for their desired careers. And you never knew when you'd run into your lucky break, or overhear a way of making your own.

So they'd come, making their way through the throng of Harley bikes in the parking lot out back. She should have known she'd been suckered when Rafe showed up with a custom stick. He'd explained pool was a game of feel, and you were only as good as your stick, and he preferred the ones that were lighter, weighing about nineteen and a half ounces.

So far they'd paid three dollars a beer to see the star of the year's hit action film and two members of the aging brat pack, plus more catsuits than she cared to count—though she was sure Rafe had made a pretty accurate one.

She was used to pool halls having a certain tawdriness about them—it was part of their appeal. But the Hollywood Athletic Club was cavernous, contemporary and well lit. For the real thing one had to go to Hollywood Billiards at Hollywood and Western, where they'd never heard of a smoke-free environment.

Still, playing pool with Rafe for the past hour had been distracting. Rafe's latest lady love had been stolen away by a surfer and, well, Anthony Gawain was making her crazy with his bandit-style kisses. She was going to have to make sure kisses were all he stole, because her heart was an all-too-willing prize.

The solution was easy enough.

She had to tell him she wasn't a sex therapist, that she'd been lying to him from the start.

Then she wouldn't have to worry about him any longer, because he'd bolt from her life. Once he found out she wouldn't be of any help with his book, he'd be off romancing someone who would.

"Pay up, lady," Rafe said, having sunk his outrageous shot. He was holding out his hand, palm up, with a pleased-as-hell grin on his face.

"Maybe your youth wasn't so misspent after all," she said, slapping the dollar bill in his palm.

"It hasn't been spent at all. I'm still a youth," he reminded her.

"Thanks ever so much for cheering me up," Nicole retorted drolly.

"You're welcome," he answered, pocketing the money.

"Okay, new bet," Nicole said, the gleam of mischief in her eyes. "If you're really good, try making this trick shot."

"That will cost you five dollars, ma'am, and then we'll grab a pizza or something. Loser buys."

"Can the 'ma'am,' shut up and shoot," Nicole grumbled, putting five dollars on the rail.

"What happened between you and Gawain anyway, to put you in such a foul mood? He find out you're not a sex therapist or something?"

"No. In fact, he wants me to help him with a survey for his book."

"You going to do it?" he asked, gripping the cue stick with his back hand directly over his rear foot.

"If I do, you're going to help me."

"Me?" Rafe said, hitting the ball above center, but moving his shoulders and messing up his follow-through, so he missed the shot.

"Yeah, we'll talk about it over that pizza you're buying me," she said, pocketing the five-dollar bill and holding out her hand for his.

"Okay, but if I'm paying, I'm choosing, and it ain't pizza," he said, paying up.

They wound up at a place he'd heard of called Venice's Queen of Cups Tearoom and Bookstore. The restaurant couldn't help but be popular in Hollywood, where movie moguls regularly consulted psychics about the future success of their pet projects—and where most movie stars had an agent, a business manager and a psychic on their payroll, none of whom they would make a move without consulting—especially the psychic.

"This place is great," Nicole said, looking around at the delicate lace curtains at the windows, the English chintz, and the in-house tarot-card readers.

"Yeah, it's pretty wild, isn't it?" Rafe said, polishing off the last of his exotic smoked-chicken hash with a bite of corn crumpet.

"You've got to help me think up some questions for this survey," Nicole said, finishing her meal soon after him.

"I can save you the trouble of doing the survey," Rafe told her. "I know the answer to the question."

"You do?"

"Sure, women want a wealthy, *sickly* octogenarian husband, and a sprinkler system that keeps a perpetually clean house, mansion, whatever."

"Rafe!"

"Well, you're a woman. You got a better answer?"

"No, a worse one."

"What is it?"

"Anthony Gawain."

"He's what *women* want—or what *you* want?"

"Unfortunately, both."

"You're real gone on him, huh?"

Nicole shook her head and put it down on the table.

He lifted her chin. "We talking lust here, or what?"

"Major lust, but it's more than that," she replied, straightening in her chair. "Anthony has this honorable streak . . . and he's sensitive."

"How does *he* feel?" Rafe asked, watching her closely.

She sighed. "Who knows?"

"I've got an idea," Rafe said. "Why don't you go browse through the transcendental book section for a minute."

"What?"

"Just do it."

Knowing humoring Rafe was easier than fighting him when he put his mind to something, she humored him.

She found out just what he was up to moments later, when he had a pretty dark-haired lady read her tea leaves.

NICOLE WAS HAVING trouble completing sentences as she sat working on her screenplay in the lounge of Le Bistro the next day before she had to start her shift. Her mind kept straying to what the tea-leaf reader had said.

*Expect the unexpected.*

And how, she wondered, was she supposed to do that?

About the only thing she could think of was that she would actually be able to complete the third act of

"Cat and Spouse"—because at the moment things weren't exactly going swimmingly. Completing her screenplay was beginning to seem like a most unreasonable expectation. She had written herself into a corner, but with the woman's tea-leaf reading in mind, she tried to concentrate on getting her characters to do her bidding, instead of wandering off on tangents of their own—tangents that had wreaked havoc with her plot line.

Nicole sighed. She supposed one was in real trouble when neither fantasy nor reality would do one's bidding. Maybe the reason she couldn't think was the stop she'd made with Rafe last night after leaving Venice's Queen of Cups Tearoom and Bookstore.

They'd topped off the evening by dropping into Le Dome for a drink. The distinctive circular bar had given them a clear view of the room, where Sherry Lansing had a regular table. Since taking over at Paramount she had been Nicole's dream choice to buy her screenplay. That night, however, Sharon Stone had been the only celebrity they saw, besides agent Swifty Lazar.

Rafe had been delighted by the eye candy Sharon provided, and had insisted Nicole try a new drink he'd heard of. She hadn't finished hers but even now, was still feeling its aftereffects.

A new employee arrived to interrupt her musing. They were exchanging pleasantries a few minutes later when Rafe blew in, looking just-showered and his usual handsome self.

"How can you look so refreshed after last night?" Nicole asked him, not bothering to keep the petty petulance from her voice.

"Clean living," he retorted with a wink at the new waitress. "And who is this pretty lady?" he asked, smiling at her.

"Elizabeth, meet Rafe Contreras. He's going to UCLA and majoring in costume design while minoring in stealing hearts—or maybe it's the other way around. In any event, be careful."

"Nicole, you're giving this lovely lady the wrong impression."

"Not. I wish someone had warned me about that drink you talked me into having last night while you were being your ever-so-charming self." Turning to Elizabeth, she explained. "My friend here had to take me home and pour me into bed after it. I overslept this morning, and I can't seem to form sentences to work on my screenplay. I don't know how I'm going to keep orders straight today. I can't even remember what stupid name that drink was called."

"It was called a Mind Eraser," Rafe supplied. "What a baby you are. You didn't even finish yours."

"That still leaves me with half a mind to kill you," she muttered. "Not everyone has a cast-iron constitution like yours, Rafe."

"Come on, Elizabeth, we've got about five minutes before our shift starts. I'll show you the ropes while Nicole, here, works her way out of her bad mood."

"I'm not in a bad mood."

Nicole watched their retreating backs, listening as Rafe turned on the charm. She shook her head. Poor Elizabeth didn't stand a chance.

She scowled at the blank page in her notebook. Rafe had been right; she was in a bad mood.

And it had nothing to do with Rafe Contreras.

Or the Mind Eraser.

Or her screenplay.

What it had to do with was Anthony Gawain.

Somehow he'd managed to get her to let down her guard, despite her prejudice against men like him.

Despite his sexy kisses, which she suspected he dispensed like Pez candies, he didn't really want her. She had to come to understand that. Anything else was just fantasy.

She couldn't fall victim to the same kind of man her father was—the kind of man her mother still hadn't learned to resist. Oh, she could see their appeal. Irresponsible men could be charming and fun to be with. But that wasn't enough for her.

She wanted a man she could depend on.

Anthony Gawain had only been dating her as a way to enlist her in his cause. His personal and selfish cause—the writing of the book he planned.

Though the look in his eyes said more, she was probably only reading into that look what she wanted to see there. She'd been lying to herself, and—worse— buying her own lie.

He wasn't the one doing the con job any longer. She had to place the blame where it really lay—with her.

She had to give up his kisses before she convinced herself she couldn't live without them. She couldn't believe she'd let things go this far.

Closing her eyes, she recalled the day at the beach. She could feel the warm sunshine on her face, smell the salt spray of the ocean, hear the water lapping. Anthony was laying her back on the beach blanket, his body covering hers. He'd lowered his lips to hers, kissing her silly...senseless.... It was he who had stopped.

Would he have stopped if they hadn't been in public?

Would she have stopped him?

Maybe it was already too late.

No.

She was an intelligent woman. She could do this. She *had* to do this.

All the beach picnic had accomplished was his getting her to agree to help him further. Despite her misgivings and doubts, she'd gotten caught up in the idea of writing a book with him.

No, that wasn't how it was. She wasn't writing a book with Anthony Gawain. She was only *researching* a book with him. She was being used.

That was what handsome, charismatic men did.

It was too bad, because the subject of what women wanted, what made relationships work in the nineties, appealed to her as a writer.

She was ashamed that her neediness was so transparent to Anthony Gawain that he'd become so sure of her. Sure that she would allow him to take advantage of her. But that was easy enough to rectify. It was a simple matter to get him out of her life.

All she had to do was tell him the truth.

Once she told him she wasn't a sex therapist, his interest in her—professional, romantic and otherwise—would disappear. He'd be gone from her life, history. It wasn't as if she was a raving beauty who could keep a man like Anthony Gawain with her looks even for a short period of time. Even if men like him always did leave eventually.

"Nicole, it's getting crazy out here," Rafe called from the doorway, balancing a tray of sandwiches high in the air.

"Be there in a sec," she promised, folding her notebook closed, stashing it and her purse in her locker and spinning the combination.

Checking her hair in the mirror, she made a face at its need of a cut. Maybe it was time she did something different with her hair. One of Rafe's friends worked at the trendy Doyle Wilson Salon, and Rafe had said he'd do hers as a freebie because he owed Rafe a favor. Rafe had gotten him a small part in the play he'd done the costumes for. Trading favors was the currency of Hollywood hopefuls, who were always short on folding money.

Nicole knew thinking about her hair was just a diversionary tactic. With a resigned sigh, she picked up her order pad and headed out to wait tables. When her shift was over, she'd call Anthony and set up a meeting to tell him the truth.

An hour and a half later, her feet hurt, her wrists ached, and her head pounded. But she was fifty bucks richer.

The place had been a mob scene—so much so that the kitchen had run out of goat cheese. The crowd had finally thinned, and now only a few late lunchers were scattered among the empty tables.

"Great job, Elizabeth," Rafe said as the three of them finished counting their tips, taking a quick break in the lounge.

"Thanks. Is it always like this?" she asked, looking a bit shell-shocked.

"About one day out of the week, wouldn't you say?" Nicole turned to Rafe for his opinion.

"That's about right. I hate it when it gets crazy, but I love the tips."

"Well, we'd better get back out there before the customers get restless," Rafe said.

Elizabeth followed his lead, but Nicole stayed behind to jot down a plot change she'd thought of while she was working.

She was just reaching for her notebook when Rafe reentered the employees' lounge.

"Ah, we've got a problem . . ." he said, as Nicole turned to see what he wanted.

"What did the kitchen run out of now?" she asked.

"The problem isn't what we don't have, it's what we do have."

"What are you talking about?"

"What we have is a certain talk-show host and his producer sitting at a table in your station."

"Rafe, that isn't funny," she said.

"I know."

There was no joking tone in his voice, she realized. "You aren't kidding, are you?"

"Nope."

"Rafe, what am I going to do?"

"You tell me."

She thought for a moment. There was a back way out, but she'd have to walk in view of the customers to use it, so that was no good. She could stay in the employees' lounge until Anthony and his producer had eaten and left. No, that wouldn't work. Rafe had just made an appointment for her to have her hair styled by his friend. She was due there in half an hour.

"Do you think you and Elizabeth can handle my station, as well as your own?" she asked, hoping her plotting was better than usual. "Most of the rush is over."

"Sure. Why?"

"I'm going to lunch."

"What?"

"I'll pretend that I've just been to the ladies' room and I'm returning to my table."

"Oh."

"You can give me a check like I've already eaten. I'll pay you, and then I'll leave."

"I get to keep the money, right?" Rafe said teasingly.

"*Rafe.*"

"What?"

"Be good."

"I am good."

"Then be better."

"Yes, ma'am."

"I was going to tell Anthony I'm not a sex therapist the next time I saw him, but I don't want him to find out this way, okay?"

"I understand. Are you ready?"

"No, but here goes. Fill Elizabeth in so this doesn't become a disaster." With that, Nicole took a deep breath, tried to calm herself and headed out to the eating area of Le Bistro.

She spotted him from the corner of her eye right away. His back was to her, as he and his producer sat near the window, at a table for four covered by a large bleached-canvas umbrella.

At her signal, Rafe came over to the table she'd pretended to return to and laid down a tab for her imaginary meal.

After glancing at it, Nicole opened her purse and took out her wallet. She handed Rafe a dollar bill and some small change.

"Thank you, miss, and please come back to see us again," he said, in case anyone was listening. Lowering his voice, he whispered, smiling, "Obviously you haven't read the amount of your bill, miss."

"A dollar thirty-five is all the tip you deserve," she said under her breath. "I hardly ate anything." She'd only given him money for appearances, and no one could tell whether she'd handed him a twenty or a one-dollar bill.

Rafe moved away to wait on a real customer, leaving Nicole to make her exit.

Gathering her courage and her purse and her notebook, she pushed back her chair and rose from the table to make her way out of the restaurant. She was going to have to pass in view of Anthony's table. There was no way around it that wouldn't draw even more attention.

She hoped he and his producer would be deep in conversation and not take notice of her.

No such luck.

"Ms. Hart, isn't it?" Mark Bates called out, spotting her leaving.

She waved, hoping that would suffice. It was ironic that someone who'd passed her over when she'd wanted to be noticed and put on Anthony's show as scheduled had spotted her when she didn't want to be noticed. It was Murphy's Law, she supposed. At least Anthony hadn't turned around yet, so maybe she could still make her escape.

"Come join us for dessert," Mark insisted, motioning her over to their table.

Anthony hadn't yet looked up from his food. She could still just nod as if she hadn't heard the producer and go on out the door.

She was about to do just that when Mark pushed back his chair and approached her.

"Ms. Hart," he said, taking her in tow. "Come say hello. You must join us for dessert. We've just ordered lemon cake with fresh strawberries. I brought Anthony over here especially to try it. They raved about it in *Los Angeles* magazine."

She was being seated before she knew it, and Rafe was taking an additional order for her. "And what would the lady like to drink?" he asked, his smile a little too wicked for Nicole's taste.

"I'll have a glass of ice water," she answered, thinking that later she could dump it on Rafe's amused head.

"Nikki," Anthony said, toying with a breadstick from the jar in the center of the table.

It struck Nicole suddenly that Anthony looked as uncomfortable as she felt. He had shot Mark a look that had clearly gone over the producer's head when he'd brought her to the table to join them.

It was clear that he hadn't intended Nicole to see the look, and the smile he turned on her in greeting appeared sincere. Perhaps the two of them had been arguing over something else, and she was reading something personal into the look that wasn't there at all.

Still, Anthony looked nervous, like a man caught out dating another woman. But that was ridiculous. He was certainly free to date any woman he chose. She didn't have any claim on him.

Besides, there wasn't anyone with him except his producer. Strange that it was Mark and not Anthony who had waylaid her on her way out of the restaurant, demanding her company. Was that it? Was there some reason Anthony hadn't wanted to see her?

No matter—she'd make some quick excuse and opt out of what her gut instinct told her was, for whatever reason, a ticklish situation. *Men!*

Anthony reached past the tiny bouquet of flowers decorating the center of the table and tapped his finger on her notebook, which she'd placed beside her purse.

"Have you been jotting down some ideas for questions for the survey?" he asked. "How's it going?"

Not wanting him to open the book and see her screenplay notes, she quickly picked up it and her purse and set them on the floor beside her chair. "It's going fine," she lied, relieved to see Rafe returning with their dessert order on a tray.

Rafe's eyes were dark with mischief as he set her dessert plate in front of her, then added her glass of ice water. "Haven't I seen you somewhere before?" he asked her.

"No," she answered, kneejerk quick, silencing him with her eyes.

"Funny, you look familiar, too," Mark said to Rafe, taking his dessert plate from him. "I know—didn't I see you the other night at Miss Olivia's?"

"Could be," Rafe answered with a nod and a grin, setting another dessert plate down on the table in front of a sulking Anthony.

"Miss Olivia's?" Nicole repeated, looking at Rafe, forgetting for the moment that she wasn't supposed to know who he was.

"Don't ask," Anthony said, shaking his head.

"It's a new club Anthony's thinking about doing a show on," Mark explained as Rafe laid down the check in front of Anthony and went to wait on another customer who'd signaled he was ready to pay.

"So, Nikki . . ." Anthony interjected, changing the subject back " . . . what sorts of questions did you come up with for the survey?"

The classical music playing in the background mixed with the sounds of Rafe and Elizabeth clearing tables. Most of the lunch customers were gone. Only two smartly dressed older women and a UPS driver doing his paperwork while he ate his sandwich remained.

"Maybe . . ." Nicole began, thinking as she talked. "Maybe you shouldn't do a made-up survey of questions at all."

"Why not? You don't think the survey is a good idea now? What changed your mind?" Anthony asked.

"Oh, I still think the survey is a good idea. It's the kind of survey you're proposing that I've changed my thinking about."

"You have another idea, I take it?"

"This is delicious," Mark said, savoring a bite of the lemon cake he'd been served.

"This place is famous for its desserts," Nicole commented without thinking. "You should try the raspberry English trifle sometime."

"You come here often, then?" Mark asked.

"Whenever I have a sweet tooth." Nicole glanced around to see where Rafe might be lurking.

"I thought you liked chocolate," Anthony said.

"No," she replied, shaking her head, beginning to feel a little more relaxed. "I don't like chocolate, I *love* chocolate. But woman does not live by chocolate alone . . . so when I've OD'd on it, I can't look at it for a while. Say, a day or two."

"What is the deal with women and chocolate, anyway?" Mark asked.

"Let's get back to the survey," Anthony said. "You were saying, Nikki . . ."

"I was saying that I thought perhaps, instead of asking questions on the survey, it might be a better idea to make it more like an essay question—say, 'What do women want?'"

Anthony cradled his chin in the vee of his thumb and forefinger. "I hadn't thought of that."

Nicole watched him take a bite of his lemon cake while he considered her idea.

"I don't think it will work," Mark objected. "It's too difficult. People won't take the time to write an essay."

Anthony ran his finger beneath the banded collar of his bronze shirt. The color set off his dark hair, which was sleeked back in a ponytail. "What do you think?" he asked, turning to Nicole and spearing a strawberry from her dessert plate.

"I think you'd better not try that again, if you don't want to lose your hand," she said. Deciding Anthony wasn't going to find out she worked at Le Bistro as a waitress instead of being a sex therapist, she started to relax. Still, she felt guilty about not telling him the truth.

Next time, she promised herself. The next time she saw Anthony, she'd tell him the truth. She could hardly do it with Mark there.

"You know what might work?" she said, getting a flash of inspiration.

"What?" the two men chorused.

"You could offer prizes. You know, like when magazines offer a free subscription."

"That's good," Anthony agreed. "We could promise to bring the winners on the television show, actually build a show around the contest."

"That would be a great publicity stunt for the book," Mark agreed. "Oh, that reminds me. I forgot to tell you, Anthony. Your agent called and left word that the contracts were in for you and Nicole to sign to coauthor the book."

"Coauthor—" Nicole echoed, her eyes narrowing.

# 9

NICOLE GRABBED HER notebook and purse and bolted from the table. She ran outside into the rain, heading for the safe anonymity of her car.

Glaring daggers at Mark, Anthony shoved his chair back and followed Nicole, calling out her name, causing heads to turn.

Nicole blessed the rain, feeling foolish and totally embarrassed that she'd been so taken in. Hot tears rolled down her cheeks blending with the raindrops.

Anthony caught up with her at her car door.

He grabbed hold of her shoulders to plead with her. "I was going to tell you, Nikki. You've got to let me explain."

"Sure, you were going to tell me, Anthony. And the sun is shining, right? Can you make every woman believe anything you say once you've drugged her with your kisses? Or is it just me who's a fool?

"Well, I may be a fool, but I'm not stupid beyond measure. You are an egotistical liar, Anthony Gawain, and I don't want to hear anything you have to say."

"Nikki, listen, I tried . . ." he began again, desperately.

"I know what you tried. I'm not listening to any more of your lies. Go ahead and author the book all by yourself, since that was obviously what you intended all along. But don't think I'm about to give you any help."

"Nikki . . ." he begged, as she pulled free of his grip and got inside her car.

He knocked on the window to get her attention, but she refused to look at him as she turned on the engine and drove away.

*Los Angeles Times*

Entertainment News:

ITEM . . . Looks like talk-show host Anthony Gawain and sex therapist Nicole Hart make a good team both on screen and off. Not only were they spotted out together at the recent Seinfeld concert, but now my sources tell me the two have been tapped to coauthor a book on the subject of their ratings-topping theme show.

"AH-AH-AH-CHOO!"

Nicole reached across the bed for the box of tissues, tossing the newspaper to the floor to join the magazines scattered there. Blowing her nose and then rubbing her burning eyes, she wondered how things had gotten this bad.

The bedroom was a mess.

Her clothes were piled right where she'd stepped out of them last night. Empty cardboard containers from a fast-food drive-through sat on a chair. Newspapers, magazines and tissues lay discarded on the bedroom floor beside the bed. Pillows and covers were half on and half off the bed from her tossing and turning.

Her life was a mess.

She still couldn't believe what had happened yesterday.

Couldn't believe the little nugget Mark had dropped into the conversation.

Throwing back the covers, she got up to get a new box of tissues and caught sight of herself in the mirror over the old-fashioned bureau. She was tempted to yank the sheet from the bed to cover the mirror before it cracked and fell to the floor in broken shards. This definitely wasn't a day to ask the "Mirror, mirror on the wall" question.

She was a mess.

No makeup, except for a few smudges of tear-stained mascara beneath her eyes. Her nose was red, her face was pale, her hair was limp. The pair of pajamas she'd dug from the bottom drawer of the bureau was at least a size too big and wrinkled, and the thick, red, slouchy socks on her feet didn't match anything but her nose.

"Ah-choo!"

She groaned and shuffled to the living room in search of another box of tissues, all the while feeling listless and sorry for herself.

The telephone rang, and the sound hurt her head.

She picked it up to silence it. It had been ringing intermittently ever since she'd gotten home yesterday afternoon. She'd been ignoring it, letting the answering machine pick up the calls. She hadn't felt like talking to anyone.

Maybe it wasn't Anthony. Maybe it was her mother calling from the Elvis wedding chapel in Las Vegas, saying she'd gotten married for the fourth time. Or maybe it was one of her sisters.

"Where have you been?"

"I've been here, Rafe."

"Then why haven't you answered the phone, or at least returned my calls?"

"I've got a cold and I don't feel good," she answered peevishly. Spying a box of tissues, she stretched the long telephone cord out straight to reach it.

"You don't feel good? Wait until you see the new entertainment column in the L.A. *Times*."

"I've already seen it."

"So how come you didn't tell me you were coauthoring a book with Gawain, instead of pretending you were only helping him research one?"

"I'm *not* coauthoring a book with Anthony Gawain," she said emphatically before sneezing.

"But the paper says—"

"I don't care what the paper says. I'm not coauthoring a book with Anthony Gawain. As a matter of fact, if you want to remain my friend, you'll never mention him again."

"What's wrong with you, Nicole? Have you got a thermometer? Maybe you should check and see if you've got a fever. You're not making any sense."

"Yes, I've got a fever, but that has nothing to do with it. And I'm starting to make sense for the first time since I met Anthony Gawain." She sniffed and blew her nose.

"Nicole ... what's going on?"

"Nothing. It's really very simple. Anthony was using me. According to his producer, he was offered— I mean, *we* were offered—a contract to write a book together based on the success of my appearance on his show. Mark thought I knew and blurted out that Anthony's agent had called to say the contracts had arrived and were waiting to be signed."

"Is that why you left Le Bistro so quickly yesterday? One minute you were there, and then I turned around and you were gone. I wondered what had happened. That's why I've been calling and leaving you messages to call me back."

"Yes."

"But why would Anthony want to cut you out of the deal? It doesn't make any sense. It's not like he needs the money or anything."

"Maybe he just didn't cotton to the idea of sharing the spotlight."

"You really believe that?"

"I don't know. But I do know that for whatever reason, he never once mentioned the contract offer to me. He only said he was planning on writing a book."

She laughed then, without humor. "Funny, isn't it, Rafe? Seems I have the last laugh, because I don't have any expertise at all to help him. He still doesn't even know that I'm not a sex therapist."

"When are you going to tell him? You *are* going to tell him, aren't you, Nicole? Nicole?"

She didn't answer.

"Nicole, are you all right? I can change my plans and come over and sit with you. I could possibly rustle up a quart of chicken soup at the deli on my way."

"I hate chicken soup," she muttered. "And I don't want any company. I want to sit here and feel sorry for myself. I don't want to have to act cheerful. I don't want to put on makeup. I just want to enjoy being sick and miserable.

"I'm coming over."

"No. I won't let you in."

"Nicole."

"I mean it. Go ahead with whatever you had planned. I'm going back to bed. I just took a cold tablet, and it's starting to make me feel sleepy already. I'll call you later, I promise."

"Are you sure?" Rafe asked, concern in his voice.

"I'm sure. But I do need you to do me one favor, if you wouldn't mind."

"If I kill Gawain, I'll have to go to prison—and there isn't much you can do with prison garb," he answered, guessing at what she wanted.

Nicole ignored his weak attempt at humor. "What I want is for you to call your friend and apologize for me missing my hair appointment. I completely forgot about it when I rushed out of Le Bistro yesterday."

"No problem," Rafe assured her. "And while I'm at it, I'll reschedule you."

"I doubt he'll want to reschedule a no-show."

"Don't worry, I'll take care of it. You take care of yourself, you hear?"

"I will. It's just a cold. I'll be okay tomorrow. Bye. Oh, and Rafe . . ."

"What?"

"I was just wondering. Where are you planning on taking Elizabeth today?"

She could hear him laughing as he hung up.

She shook her head. No single woman in L.A. was safe around him. Hanging up herself, she pushed up the sleeves of her pajamas for what seemed like the hundredth time.

In the kitchen she opened the refrigerator and looked inside hopefully. The cool air escaping as she stood there felt good against her feverish skin. She took a couple of swigs from a plastic bottle of mineral water. Then, replacing it, she considered what else was available to her.

A slice of cheese in plastic wrap curling up on one end, a couple of stalks of celery looking as limp as she felt, and a jar of pickles.

She closed the door on a weary sigh.

Schlepping back to the bedroom clutching her box of tissues, she climbed into bed. After setting the box of tissues beside her on the bed, she picked up a fashion magazine and began leafing through the glossy pages, her half-shuttered eyes barely focusing.

Long skirts were coming back in style.

So were platform shoes. Yuck!

She flipped back to the last page of the magazine, where the horoscope for the month was usually printed. Running her finger down the page, she stopped when she came to her sign and began reading.

You'll experience love of the giving kind. Jupiter's transit through your eighth house brings a heightened sexual intimacy.

Great. That explained it.

The stars were against her.

She was the one doing the giving, all right. And her heightened sexual intimacy was there for the taking. No wonder it had been so easy for Anthony to waltz right in and take what he wanted.

She wondered what sign Anthony was.

He was most probably a Leo—king of the jungle and all that, his mane of hair a dead giveaway. And he had the confidence to attract wealth and the limelight.

"Ah-ah-ah-choo!"

She closed the magazine and reached for a tissue to blow her nose.

Anthony Gawain. Why had she let herself fall for him? He was self-centered, self-indulgent and immature. A pleasure seeker. She'd read some women purposely picked Mr. Wrong to avoid marriage. That way they could wait for the perfect fantasy man who didn't exist in reality. Was that why she preferred fantasy? Probably. In fantasy there was no opening oneself up to rejection and pain.

Why had she fallen for Anthony Gawain?

The answer was easy enough: He wasn't safe.

He was a challenge. He met her head-on, and the resulting skirmishes were exciting. Other, safer men bored her.

She was like her mother, no matter how she tried to deny it. They both had a really low boredom threshold.

Well, she hadn't been bored. She'd give Anthony that.

But with a dangerous man, the letdown, when it came and it always came—was a killer.

Her head ached too much for her to think about it.

Hot tea. She needed some hot tea with honey to clear her head so that she could make an attempt at working on her screenplay. She wanted to see if the notes she'd jotted down at Le Bistro would pan out. If she was on the right track, she would be able to clear up the hole in her plot and finish "Cat and Spouse."

On her way back from the kitchen with the tea ten minutes later, she noticed and gave in to the message light flickering on her answering machine. Pressing the Replay button, she took a sip of the hot liquid, letting the steam clear her nasal passageways to make her breathing easier.

*Beep* . . .

"Nicole, are you home? We need to talk, call me when you get in. I'll be at the studio. The number is 555-6541."

She recognized Anthony's voice.

*Beep* . . .

"Nicole. It's Rafe. Where'd you go so quickly? Is anything wrong? Give me a call."

*Beep* . . .

"Nicole, come on, pick up the phone. We need to talk. Nicole . . . are you there?"

Anthony got impatient when he didn't get his way, she thought with a sniffle and a smile.

*Beep* . . .

"Hello . . . It's Rafe. My phone was off the hook for a little while. If you called, call me back. If you didn't, call me anyway. I want to find out about your lunch date. Elizabeth quit. . . . Don't . . . I'll talk to you later, Nicole."

*Beep* . . .

"Nikki, pick up the damn phone!"

This time she laughed out loud, sloshing tea from her cup into her saucer. From the sound of his roar, it appeared the lion was getting just a little testy.

*Beep* . . .

"Nicole, it's Wendy. Have you heard from Mother lately? She hasn't gone and done anything foolish—well, *really* foolish—has she? Give me a call."

Nicole hit the Replay button.

Her sister Wendy didn't approve of their mother's rodeo cowboy, and Nicole wasn't up to hearing about it today. She'd call Wendy back tomorrow, when she felt better, she decided, heading back to the bedroom.

An hour or so later, she'd made progress with a rough draft of the ending of her screenplay, but her eyes were starting to grow heavy.

The pen slipped from her fingers as she drifted off to sleep.

She began dreaming. . . .

*She was in a pool hall after hours—the intimate kind that had a neon sign in the window. She was closing up for the night, racking the balls in the center of the tables.*

*The door to the street opened, and she turned to say they were closed for the night. The words stuck in her throat when she saw who had entered.*

*In the billiard circles he was known as The Ice Man. He played seldom, and only for big stakes. While he was often challenged, he'd never been beaten when he chose to play. Like a gunslinger, he was the one to beat if you were looking to make your reputation.*

*Though he didn't play in fancy pool halls or tournaments, he had no shortage of challengers. When he chose to play, he played one-on-one, one game, winner take all.*

*No one knew anything about him. He was mysterious, as ethereal as smoke.*

*Rumor had it he came from a wealthy, influential family. . . that he was the black sheep. There'd been some trouble involving an older woman—a woman who should have been forbidden to him.*

*One had only to look at him to see that he didn't play by anyone's rules. He was a maverick, maybe even dangerous. His glossy black hair was slicked back in a ponytail. It played up the great bone structure of his aristocratic face.*

*A small silver cross studded one ear.*

*He wore a black leather jacket tossed over a gray cashmere sweater, paired with jeans and flat-heeled, soft leather boots with a metal-tipped toepiece.*

*Finding her voice, she finally asked, "What do you want?"*

*His gaze slid over her body, slowly taking inventory, staking a claim. When his green eyes returned to her face, their look held a challenge.*

*"I've come to play."*

*Her eyes widened, and she took a quick gasp of breath.*

He held up the black lacquer case that contained his custom cue stick. Upping the level of tension, he said, "Straight pool. I call every shot."

She swallowed dryly, wondering—knowing—what the stakes were. And knowing his level of skill. He'd dusted the very best. He was the perfect example of the traveling player, always seeking the ultimate game.

Advancing further into the dimly lit pool hall, he shrugged off his black leather jacket and pushed up the sleeves of his gray cashmere sweater, all the while holding her with his eyes, the quiet around them cocooning them.

He snapped open the black lacquer case and took out his cue, fitting it together. She felt herself flush when she saw the notches on the stick. It was rumored there was one for every time he'd won. It was clear he was a man who kept score. A man who relished winning above all else.

A careful, exacting man, he chalked his cue, measuring her response to him while he did. Then, lifting the wooden triangle corralling the brightly colored balls, he set it aside and lined up his stick for the break shot.

It was a good break, one made with the sure skill of a surgeon's hands. In short order he called each ball and sank it in the pocket he called out. He was obviously an expert at running the balls, not to mention the game.

Looking up after sinking the last black ball, he considered her. His look sent a shiver of excitement racing along her spine.

"Do you concede my victory?" he asked, resting his hip on the rim of the pool table and tossing the eight ball in the air, then catching it with one hand.

"I haven't had my chance to play," she said, shaking her head no.

"You won't get one. I can go all night. I never miss a shot," he assured her, cocky as hell.

"Hasn't anyone ever ruined your concentration—made you miss a shot?" she asked, biting her lower lip.

He squeezed the black ball in his hand, flexing his long fingers. "No one," he answered.

"Then we'll have to make the game more interesting, won't we?" she said, first leaning one hip on the edge of the pool table, then stretching out to rest the length of her body provocatively on the rim. "Rack 'em, cowboy," she challenged, laying down the gauntlet.

"Yes, ma'am." Standing, he corralled the balls into a perfect triangle, then paused to chalk his cue. "You know, pretty women usually bring me luck."

She didn't respond, just smiled her secret smile as he hit the cue ball, medium speed, dead center, setting up a perfect field.

He studied the table, assessing the best play. "You're in my way."

"Call your shot," she said, waiting to move.

"Purple stripe off the side into the left rear pocket."

Straightening, Nicole slipped from the table, allowing him access to his shot.

"Just a minute," she said, stopping him as he prepared to make his shot.

"What is it?"

She moved to the end of the pool table, where she proceeded to hoist herself up on the mother-of-pearl-inlaid rosewood rail. As she stretched out along the rail, right where he would have to make his shot, her skirt inched up provocatively.

The Ice Man was beginning to sweat. She looked him straight in the eye and said, "Let's see how good your stroke really is."

He raised his black-lacquer cue stick, studying the silver accents, and rested his hand on the smooth felt table, sliding the stick back and forth, preparing for the shot.

Just as he put English on the ball to sink the shot, she said, "I hope your nickname isn't Fast Anthony or anything."

*He missed the shot.*

*She smiled, every inch the coquette. "You lose."*

*Taking his time, he unscrewed his cue and put it back into its case. Then, turning back to the pool table, he clicked the balls together, sweeping them from its surface.*

*"Wrong sweetheart—I win," he said, climbing onto the pool table.*

*"What—what do you think you're doing?"*

*He motioned her forward with the crook of his finger, a wicked gleam in his eyes. "This is a pickup game, isn't it?"*

*Flicking open the buttons of her blouse, he uncovered her breast and began to suck gently on its pink peak. . . .*

From what seemed a great distance came the insistent peal of her doorbell.

# 10

NICOLE AWOKE SLOWLY, a warm flush covering her body. Her eyes fluttered open, and she stretched, feeling warm, fuzzy, and very, very sexy.

The doorbell pealed again. That was what had roused her, she remembered now, wondering who would have the nerve to call on her in the middle of the night. And then she saw the sunlight streaming in the French door and realized it was daylight. She'd fallen asleep while working on her screenplay.

The doorbell pealed again.

It had to be Rafe, bringing her chicken soup, mothering her.

Throwing back the covers, she caught sight of herself in the mirror over the maple dresser. The mirror still wasn't doing her any favors. It was going to take more than chicken soup, she muttered to herself, patting down a clump of hair that she'd slept on wrong.

When her feet hit the floor, she looked down to see that she had lost one of her warm red socks, and went on a reconnaissance mission beneath the covers until she came up with it. After putting it on, she ran her hand through her hair, trying to straighten it a bit. She rubbed her eyes and yawned. Hazy images from her dream came back to her.

The doorbell pealed again.

As soon as she let Rafe in, she was going to kill him for awakening her from her dream just as it was getting really good— Well, bad....

She smiled wickedly, recalling certain sexy details.

The doorbell pealed again just as she reached it.

"Okay, okay, keep your pants on," she muttered. "Or maybe not," she said with a silly giggle, unlocking the door.

"I thought I told you I didn't want—"

It wasn't Rafe.

It was the dark-haired man with the ponytail.

The bad man.

The good dream had turned into a nightmare. She slammed the door shut.

"Nikki, let me in."

"Go away."

"Nikki ..."

"Go away," she said, walking back to her bedroom.

He rang the doorbell again just as she sat down on the bed. She covered her ears with her hands. How could he still be ringing her doorbell, when he'd seen her looking her very worst? Why didn't he go away and let her die of embarrassment in peace?

But no, the doorbell kept up its insistent pealing.

She ignored it, climbing into bed and pulling the covers over her head, making it and the world go away.

It worked.

The doorbell stopped ringing.

She hadn't really wanted it to. What she'd wanted more than anything was to believe that more than beauty mattered to a man. To one particular man, at least. But that was just a foolish hope.

Anthony Gawain didn't care about her.

He'd only come after her because he needed her expertise—expertise she didn't have. Wasn't that a laugh?

Somehow she didn't feel like laughing.

She wrinkled her brow, listening intently. What was that sound she'd just heard? Had she imagined it? she wondered as she continued listening.

Nothing. The house was silent.

She was about to get out from under the covers when she heard it again.

The sound of footsteps.

Oh, no!

She'd closed the door on Anthony, but she hadn't locked it. He was inside the house.

She had to hide, quickly. Silly, she reminded herself, she was already hiding.

"Nikki?"

She remained quiet beneath the covers. He'd go away if she didn't answer him. Why was her heart beating so loudly? He'd hear it. She held her breath as the footsteps came nearer the bedroom.

"Nikki?"

She heard him pause in the doorway of the bedroom.

She held her breath, trying not to make a sound or a move. Her nose began to tickle. She rubbed it, trying to hold back the sneeze she felt building.

"Ah-ah-choo!"

Anthony's rich laughter filled the air.

"You can come out now, I've found you," he said finally.

"Go away."

"I'm not going away, Nikki. We have to talk, you and I."

"I don't want to talk," she retorted with the petulance of a recalcitrant child.

"Okay, then. Just listen," Anthony said patiently. "I want to explain. You ran out yesterday without giving me a chance to explain."

Nikki reconsidered. If she stayed beneath the covers, he couldn't see her. Maybe if she listened to him he would go away and leave her alone. Not that she would believe anything he had to tell her.

"Okay, I'll listen," she agreed, her voice muffled by the covers.

"What?"

"Go ahead."

"Nikki, I can't understand what you're saying. You'll have to come out from beneath the covers."

"No."

"Nikki...I'm waiting. Stop being so obstinate. I'm not leaving until you come out from under there and listen, like an adult, to what I have to say."

That hurt. So she wasn't behaving very adultlike. She didn't have to if she didn't want to. And she didn't want to. If she wanted to behave like a child, then she could. And nothing Anthony Gawain said or did could change her mind.

"Nikki, you're behaving like a child."

She threw off the covers. "I am not."

"What's wrong with you?" he asked. Then, seeing her up close, he said, "You've caught a cold, haven't you? Probably got a fever, as well. That would explain why you're acting like this."

"I'm . . . ah-ah-choo!"

"You are too sick. You must have caught cold when we were standing arguing in the rain yesterday."

"I'm...I'm..." She sneezed. "I'm fine." She reached for a tissue. "You just go ahead." She waved the tissue in the air. "Explain and then leave."

"I'm not leaving now. You need someone to take care of you."

"I don't need anyone to take care of me. I am not a child," she insisted, blowing her nose.

"Maybe. But you are sick."

"I only have a little cold."

"Well, we need to make you more comfortable. First, if you'll get out of bed and sit on that chair over there for a minute, I'll put fresh linens on the bed and it will make you feel better."

"Oh, and I suppose you're going to give me a nice warm bath, too," she snapped, regretting her words the minute they left her tongue.

"If you like . . ." The words sounded intimate and sexy and brought back her erotic dream.

Though she was blushing, she still managed to glare at him.

"Okay, out of bed," he ordered, advancing on her.

She backed off to the other side, letting him intimidate her.

He stripped the bed in short order and went to the linen closet in the hall for fresh sheets. She also heard him making a phone call, but she couldn't make out who he was talking to in hushed tones.

Probably he was telling a girlfriend he'd be a little late picking her up for a date because he'd been delayed unexpectedly. Either that or he was calling his producer to set up meeting at Miss Olivia's later. Or, even more likely, he was meeting one of Miss Olivia's girls, she thought sulkily—which was ludicrous, because she hated Anthony Gawain. What he did was no concern of hers.

And that was just fine with her.

He returned with the fresh linen and made up the bed—something she was actually surprised to find he knew how to do, what with his privileged background. Feeling exposed, she climbed back beneath the covers.

"Okay, you can go now," she said ungraciously.

"Not before I tell you a bedtime story."

"Funny, you don't look like Mother Goose." The Big Bad Wolf was more like it, she thought to herself. She didn't say it, figuring that would be pushing her luck.

"There once was a young boy who loved his mother very much," he began.

"Is this going to be a Shakespearean fairy tale?"

"Just be quiet and listen."

She fluffed the pillow behind her back and waited.

The sooner he said his piece, the sooner he'd be gone. She wasn't just having a bad-hair day; she doubted she'd ever looked worse in her life.

And Anthony had probably never looked better.

He had on a black-and-jade crinkle-fabric jogging suit that set off his green eyes and dark coloring. If he had indeed been jogging, he hadn't worked up a sweat.

And here she was, looking like she'd gone five rounds with a wild tiger—and lost.

Anthony turned his back to her, then began speaking in a voice not much above a whisper. "To prove to you that bad judgment is the only thing I'm guilty of in waiting to tell you about the offer to coauthor the book, I'm going to tell you a secret that no one else knows about me."

Why wasn't he looking at her? And what was this secret that was so shocking he couldn't face her? Nicole wondered, feeling her anger receding.

"When I was nine," Anthony continued, "I overheard my mother in conversation with a friend." Anthony laughed then, a rueful, choking sound. "I guess what they say about eavesdropping is true: You never hear anything good." He took a deep breath and continued. "To make a long story short, I found out that day that I'm not really a Gawain."

"You were adopted?" Nicole asked.

"No, I'm a bastard. And my mother is a bitch." His condemnation was harsh and pained. "You see, she had a lover, and she failed to mention to her husband that his firstborn was another man's child."

"Anthony... I'm... I'm so sorry. You must have been..."

"Yes, I was," he said, turning to face her. "But I learned from it. I learned how deceitful a woman can be. Before I met you, I'd given up hope there was a woman who didn't want a man she could dupe. A woman who didn't want to use a man to get what she wanted.

"I liked that you didn't cater to me when we met, the way other women did. But then, later, I got to wondering if maybe that was your angle. That you were maybe a little smarter than the others, but just as mercenary.

"That's why, when the offer came in for us to coauthor a book, I waited to tell you. I wanted time to get to know you. I didn't want to fall in love, only to find you were just using me as a path to being a celebrity therapist. I wanted you to want me for myself."

Nicole couldn't believe what she was hearing.

Anthony Gawain really did care about her. He'd proved it by telling her, trusting her with, the secrets of his past.

"What are you saying, exactly?" she asked finally.

"I'm saying that I want you to coauthor the book with me. I have always wanted you to coauthor the book with me, Nikki."

He started straightening the room, putting the newspapers and magazines in a stack, and then he came to sit beside her on the bed.

"Please say that you'll do it."

Now was the time for her to tell him that she wasn't a sex therapist. But she couldn't. She'd have to work up the nerve first.

"I'll do it," she agreed. She knew that not telling him the truth was wrong, but she didn't want to lose what they might have together.

She *would* tell him.

But not just yet.

He smiled with pleasure at her answer. Taking her hand, he kissed the inside of her wrist. "Now...about that bath," he said, his eyes dancing.

She shook her head, pulling her hand back from him. "No bath."

He put his hand to her forehead.

"You feel warm. I'm going to run you some bath-water."

"You do and I'll run."

"*From* me or *to* me, Nikki?"

He was impossible. He had all the right questions and all the right answers.

She, on the other hand, had none of the willpower she needed to resist his very charming self. After the sexy dream she'd had about him, he didn't stand a chance of getting away untouched.

"Okay, run the bath," she said, giving in to what they both wanted.

It was obvious that her sudden capitulation surprised him.

It was there in his eyes. He trailed his finger down her nose. "Tell me, Nikki, are you always such a good little girl?"

Holding his intent gaze, she grabbed his finger, slipping it into her mouth and sucking it ever so slowly. Then she removed it, her eyes dancing. "Define 'good.'"

"Okay," he said on a ragged breath. "Maybe I could be persuaded to forget about that bath."

She laughed. "And here I thought you were such a tough guy."

"Well, I wouldn't want to disappoint a lady," he said, flipping back the covers.

"What do you think you're doing?" she demanded.

"Why, I'm carrying you off to your bath, Ms. Hart," he replied, scooping her up in his strong arms. "Scream all you like, my pretty, but I've instructed the castle guards to turn a deaf ear."

She beat on his back with her fists, playing along. "Put me down, you beast!"

To her surprise, he did as she requested. "Okay, but can I watch?" he asked, all wicked villain.

"No."

"No?"

She shook her head, emphasizing her negative reply.

"*No?*" he repeated, his voice threatening and deep. "So much for being a gentleman, then," he said, scooping her back up in his arms.

"Okay, okay. You can help," she agreed, giggling.

"Yes!"

"Anthony..."

"Umm..." he murmured, nuzzling her neck as he carried her to the bathroom.

"I was kidding."

"No way."

"Way."

"No fair."

"I told you to get that stress test, remember."

"Nikki..."

"What?"

"I got it."

"No way."

"Way."

Lowering himself to sit on the edge of the claw-foot bathtub with her on his lap, he reached to turn on the old-fashioned white ceramic faucets, adjusting the flow of hot and cold water until he had the temperature just right.

Nicole reached across him to the shelf on the wall for a bottle of apple-scented bubble bath. She up-ended a couple of capfuls into the water cascading from the faucets, icing the water with foamy bubbles.

Putting the cap back on the bubble bath, she returned it to the shelf.

As she turned back, her eyes collided with his. She felt the heat rise in her face—and remembered with sudden clarity just how awful she looked.

"You can go now," she said, starting to rise from his lap.

The cream-colored walls of the small bathroom seemed to close in, and the steam rising from the bathwater gave the small space a hothouse effect. She could smell his need, could feel hers. The atmosphere was overpoweringly erotic. It was like feeling the soft leather of the back seat of a car against your naked body—in a crowded parking lot.

Though there was no danger of anyone seeing them, there was the danger of showing too much.

The danger of exposure.

The danger of revealing more than skin.

"I'm not going anywhere, Nikki. I'm here to make you feel better."

And she was entirely certain that he could make her feel better. Better than she'd ever felt in her life.

And then worse. To have him once would be like taking an addictive drug just once. She knew she'd crave him forever more.

But the temptation to chance it was too strong. Her desire was too strong.

His kiss, when it came, overrode her resistance. It sucked her into a whirlpool of desire. It was a scorching kiss so hot it left her dizzy. She was melting as he nibbled kisses down her neck and began undoing her pajama buttons with his teeth.

She moaned, thrusting her fingers into his mane of thick, glossy hair, arching her neck as hot waves of need swelled.

She was helpless with want.

He pulled her pajama top back, slipping it from her shoulders and pinning her arms, lathing her collarbone with the flat of his tongue as he worked his way to her breast.

Cupping the soft fullness with one hand, he blew his warm breath over the peak, making it pucker with need. And then dream merged with reality as he began to suck gently at her breast, concentrating on its pink tip with his tongue. All the while, his long fingers kneaded and squeezed, adding to the exquisite sensations he aroused.

She cried out softly.

He lifted his head and smiled at her. "Look," he said, covering her breast with his hand. "You were made for me—a perfect fit."

She looked down to see his tanned hand against her pale, rosy skin and flushed.

He chuckled and shook his head. "I can't believe you keep doing that."

"The water must be getting cold," she said, turning away, suddenly embarrassed.

"Well, then, we'll just have to get on with it, won't we?" He bit her bare shoulder lightly.

Lifting a fluffy washcloth from the shelf, he dipped it in the water beneath the thick surface of bubbles, squeezed it out and then soaped it. "Okay, now close your eyes real tight,"

She did as he asked without argument, all the resistance having gone out of her. He'd kissed her senseless.

A moment later, she felt the warm soapy cloth on her face as he began washing her. Taking care, he moved from her face to her neck to her arms. Her breasts felt bereft when he rinsed out the washcloth.

But he resoaped it and returned to them. When he began sliding the warm, soapy cloth over her breasts, she whimpered. The touch of the washcloth against her tender breasts was like that of a cat's tongue who'd just lapped up a bowl of rich cream.

She was purring beneath his touch.

Next thing she knew, she'd be rubbing up against him, she thought with chagrin.

She couldn't open her eyes, because she'd get soap in them, so the effect was dreamlike. She could feel his touch, but she couldn't see him. And if she couldn't see him, it wasn't really happening.

Liar, her body told her.

"These are cute as hell," he said, tugging her red socks from her feet. Then he was tugging on her pajama bottoms.

"I . . ." She started to object on a quick intake of breath, but it was too late. The bottoms were already pooled at her feet along with her pajama top. She could feel the steamy air caressing her naked body.

She started to step away from the pajamas, but then she heard him splashing the washcloth in the tub.

"Stay," he ordered.

To her surprise, she found herself complying, obeying his command. That was not a good sign.

He kissed the nape of her neck and began washing her back with sure, efficient strokes. That finished, he dropped the washcloth in the tub.

"Here—take my hand," he said, holding it next to hers.

She brushed his hand away. "I can get in the tub all by myself," she insisted.

"But I don't want you in the tub just yet. Take my hand, Nikki," he said, rinsing the washcloth and wiping her face clean of soap.

She blinked her eyes open. Disoriented for a moment, she took his hand.

"This isn't fair," she said. "You take off *your* top."

Releasing her hand, he unzipped his top and tossed it aside. "Any more requests you'd like me to fulfill?" he asked, testing her.

She shook her head no.

"Then take my hand and step up here," he said, patting the lid of the commode.

"What?"

"Just do it."

She considered him a moment, then did as he wanted.

"Now stand still," he ordered, soaping the washcloth once again.

She swallowed and closed her eyes as he began sliding the warm, soapy cloth over her abdomen and her hips and then down the outsides of her legs. When he started at the insides of her ankles and slowly soaped his way up, she began to tremble.

"Here—slide down and sit on the tank," he said, dropping the washcloth back into the tub of bathwater. "Wait. First let me put this towel here for you to sit on, so you won't slip off."

She waited, then let him settle her on top of the tank. Her eyes still closed, she listened for him to rinse the washcloth in the bathwater and then begin to rinse her. Her skin felt alive with wanting his touch.

But all she heard was the sound of him hopping on one foot and then the other, followed by the whisper of the crinkly fabric of his pants falling to the tile floor.

He was naked, she knew.

She wanted desperately to look.

But she couldn't.

She was such a wimp.

She could barely breathe. And then she felt his hands on her knees and gasped as he separated them so that he could sit down on the lid of the commode, facing her. Lifting her legs, he placed them over his shoulders, then began nipping and kissing the insides of her thighs.

Beneath the backs of her knees she felt his powerful shoulders, felt them move up the backs of her thighs as he leaned closer. She felt herself lifting . . . yearning for the caress of his mouth.

He had aroused her so thoroughly that she was beyond reason. Beyond shame, embarrassment or modesty. Beyond thinking of anything but the fact that she wanted his mouth on her, his tongue—

"That's it, sweetheart, come to me," he said hoarsely, his hands slipping beneath her to bring her to him.

"Yes!" she cried out the moment his mouth closed over her, the hot touch of his tongue bringing her to a wild, sweet, shattering orgasm.

Her hands clenched and unclenched in his dark hair as she panted, trying to catch her breath as she pulsated against his mouth.

When her ragged breathing became even, she blinked open her eyes and looked down at him. This time she didn't feel a flush of embarrassment heating her face. She felt only the glow of contentment lighting it. She bit her lip and smiled at him ruefully.

He grinned back—big time.

With a very naughty wink, he said, "Told ya I'd make you feel better."

"You're one bad man, Anthony Gawain...." She closed her eyes again and leaning her head back against the wall, all her little energy spent.

He stood, and she opened her eyes to see that he was aroused. In fact, the smooth, satiny hardness of him was demanding attention.

"Do you have anything, Nikki?" he asked, his meaning sure and caring.

She shook her head no.

"Neither do I. But I remember passing a drugstore near here. Why don't you go ahead and finish your bath? I'll be right back."

"But how can you be certain they're open?" she asked.

He at least had the decency to look sheepish.

"I called . . . earlier," he answered truthfully.

After he left, she slipped into the tub of bubble bath. Scooping a handful of bubbles, she blew the white foam into the air.

"You're a bad man, Anthony Gawain. . . ." she said with a sigh.

And then she smiled.

ANTHONY CHECKED THE time on the dash in his Jeep.

It had taken him twenty minutes to shop, from the time he'd pulled into the parking lot of the sprawling drugstore. There had been only one cashier on duty, and the place had been jammed with customers.

Murphy's Law had required there be some person ordering reprints in odd sizes and lots to gum up the works.

Unlike the others in line, he'd managed to hold onto his temper. But then, he was feeling mellow, as well as wired. On the seat beside him was the reward for his patience—a grocery sack filled to the brim. A quick check of Nicole's refrigerator hadn't been very encouraging.

At least now, he had the makings of breakfast from the drugstore's convenience section.

He was a very hungry man, with appetites to be sated. Reaching into the grocery bag, he pulled out a smaller sack, double-checking to make sure the harried cashier hadn't overlooked it.

He let out a sigh as he made a left turn. He was all set. And just to make extra sure, he pulled out the insurance package he'd added at the last minute.

A giant bag of M & M's.

He knew they melted in your mouth, but he thought maybe he could improve on that....

He was feeling the anticipatory rush of a senior prom night as he let himself into Nicole's place.

"I'm back!" he called out, in a great imitation of a popular action movie star. Setting the grocery sack down in the kitchen, he shoved the contents in the refrigerator. Then, unzipping his jogging suit as he went, he headed for the bathroom. He couldn't wait to join Nicole in the bath.

An empty tub greeted him. For an instant he felt as if he'd arrived at the gym on the wrong night for the prom.

"Nikki?" he called out.

Silence echoed back at him.

She wasn't in the living room, either, so he headed for the bedroom, rearranging his plan. So he'd take a quick shower instead....

"Nikki, I—"

She was already in bed. Her hair was still damp on the pillow.

Moving closer, he saw that she was deliciously naked—and fast asleep.

Resigned, he headed for the shower—a cold one.

He was a grown man, and he knew all about pleasures delayed. In the morning they'd have a Continental breakfast in bed—Colombian coffee, French toast, Swedish massage, French kisses ...

# 11

THE SMELL OF BUTTERY French toast and the distinctive aroma of fresh coffee woke Nicole. She yawned wide and stretched. And then realized she was naked.

Where were her baggy pajamas?

Blinking her eyes open, she saw that the late show was on TV and Anthony Gawain was serving her breakfast, wearing only an apron with reindeer on it.

She closed her eyes. She had to be dreaming.

When she opened her eyes again, the food would be gone. Anthony would be gone. And the TV would have a test pattern on it.

"Nikki, your food is getting cold, and I'm getting—" he untied the apron "—hot."

It wasn't a dream.

"Uh . . ." She was actually speechless.

"Are you feeling better?" he asked, cutting her a piece of French toast and lifting it, dripping with maple syrup, to her lips.

She chewed slowly. It all came back to her as she looked at him. He'd stolen her heart, and her breath.

He raked his hand through his unbound hair at her scrutiny.

She licked the syrup from her lips, slowly, absently.

"Like what you see?" he asked, bracing himself on his elbow as he lay across the bed.

"What do you think?" she asked.

"I think I need a little private therapy," he said.

She slid her hand across his chest, and down the flat planes of his belly, then molded her hand around him.

"Is this what you had in mind?" she asked, squeezing and releasing her grip as she stroked him.

"It'll—it'll do for starters," he choked out.

"Umm . . ." she murmured, dipping her head to his lap, her tongue flicking and retreating, hardening him to steel.

He seized her hand on a groan of pleasure, bringing her palm up to kiss it, then lick it, the look in his eyes hot and electric.

"I want to bury myself inside you," he vowed. His kiss was deep and possessive, thrilling her, making clear the claim he was staking.

"Oh, yes," she whispered, her breath warm, her voice trembly against his ear.

"I want you now," she said, pushing him onto his back.

"Wait a minute—" he started to object, rising on his elbows.

"Shut up and pay attention," she instructed. "I'm grouchy when I wake up unless I get my way." She moved over him, taking him inside her with sweet, urgent possession.

He fell back on the bed.

"You've got...my...ah-h-h...attention," he groaned, reaching to fill his hands with her upturned breasts, kneading them as she moved. His jaw clenched as she built a slow, sensual rhythm, carrying him with her until they sped out of control and over the edge into ecstasy.

"Nikki!" he cried out, drowning her moans as she collapsed against him, breathing hard, shuddering with an ebbing orgasm.

They lay entwined for long moments, contented, happy, spent.

On the television a trailer was running for the new movie, *Bodyguard*. Whitney Houston was singing the theme song, "I Will Always Love You."

It lent a tender poignancy to what they'd just shared, what they'd said with their bodies, Nicole thought, swept up in the lyrics.

She stirred finally, raising her body from his.

"I'm hungry," she announced.

"Worked up an appetite, did you?" he asked, teasing her.

Nodding, she trailed a playful finger down his slick chest. "I figured a man who wore a jogging suit ought to at least work up a little sweat."

"And now that I've allowed you to have your way with me, you're going to feed me, right?"

"Feed you?"

"Yeah, you know, as in I cooked, you feed."

"Funny," she said, kissing the tip of her finger and planting it on his lips. "I thought I just cooked."

He reached for the plate of still-warm French toast. "Let's call it a tie and feed each other," he said, offering her a fork.

By the time they'd finished their French toast and coffee, Letterman was on television. Plumping up a mound of pillows behind them, they sat back to watch the show, all the while nuzzling, kissing and enjoying the afterglow of their impromptu lovemaking.

Letterman's guest was Chelsea Stone, the bad girl of rock and roll. She had been out of the limelight for six months, recovering from throat surgery, and was debuting her new song.

"Now there's a woman of the nineties," Anthony said. "She competes toe-to-toe with the bad boys of rock and roll, and she takes no prisoners."

"I know. I admire her because she knows what she wants and goes after it."

"Speaking of what women want . . ." Anthony segued. "We need to talk about your ideas for the book we're coauthoring."

*Coauthoring.* Nicole knew she should tell him the truth right then. She couldn't coauthor the book with him, because she wasn't a sex therapist, as both he and the publisher believed.

This charade had gone on far too long—far longer than she'd planned. He'd just presented her with the perfect opportunity to tell him the truth. But she didn't have it in her to ruin this night. It was too special to her.

In the morning she'd tell him. She'd make him understand the reasons for her deception . . . expose her fears . . . make him forgive her. . . .

IT WAS TWO IN THE morning. Letterman was over, the television was off, but she and Anthony were still deep in discussion about the proposed book. They'd skipped from subject to subject until Nicole blurted out the bottom line.

"You know, Anthony, what men don't ever seem to want to admit is that maybe women have a reason for being deceitful."

"Yeah, they enjoy it," he said darkly.

"Okay, so maybe some do. But I'd wager the majority don't. And in my opinion, men have only themselves to blame for women's deceit."

"What?"

"Women have had to use deceit to get their needs taken care of. That's true any time you have an unequal division of power—especially economic power. If a person doesn't have an economic base, they can't bail out of an intolerable situation. They can't even bargain effectively."

"Why not?"

"Haven't you ever heard of the golden rule?"

"Sure . . . Do unto others as—"

"No, not that one, the other one. 'He who has the gold, rules.' Period. The final verdict always rests with the person—that is, the male—who is in the position of power."

"You don't really believe that. Lots of women live wonderfully fulfilling lives without ever joining the work force. They have happy marriages with husbands who love and pamper them."

"I'm sure that's true. But not in every case. And there is a flaw to that system."

"Which is?"

"A woman's life is only as good as the man she chooses—usually with the wisdom of a teenager, as that's when most women meet the man they will marry. If the man they choose is a good and decent man and a loving provider, then it can and does work wonderfully. But if she chooses unwisely or has limited or no choices, then her life can be hell."

"Aha, but men can make the same mistakes, choosing unwisely when they're young," Anthony countered.

"Yes, they can. But they have the economic power to change their situation. When men divorce, they become basically single again, unencumbered by the responsibility of children. They may pay child support, but they aren't responsible for their day-to-day care. On the other hand, when women divorce, they become the new poor. While men's life-styles improve or remain the same, women's plummet."

"So you're saying basically that you think what women want is equality."

Nicole adjusted the pillow behind her and thought for a moment. "You know what I think women want more than anything?"

Anthony narrowed his eyes. "Are we talking physical proportions here?"

She threw the pillow she'd been adjusting at him. "No, fool, you men are all so paranoid about that, and we could care less. A good lover is more than the sum of his 'parts.' What women really want, I think, is a wife."

"A wife!"

Nicole nodded. "What women are in the nineties is tired. We're sandwiched in between taking care of parents and children, or we're new mothers with careers and children, or we're single women trying to earn what it takes two people in a marriage to earn to stay afloat economically."

"That's because women want it all. The old way—"

"Forget it," Nicole said, interrupting him. "Women are never going back to washing their clothes on rocks in the creek and lying back and saying it was good for them when it wasn't. That's a man's fairy tale. A Grimm fairy tale. Hard economic times are stressing us all to the max, but one thing women aren't about to give up is the economic gains they've made."

"But what about men? It isn't easy for us. In case you haven't noticed, we've been dropping like flies."

"That's another book," Nicole rebutted.

"Good idea," he agreed. "I think I'll talk to Mark about planning a show on it for the next sweeps-week period."

Nicole yawned.

"You don't think it's a good idea?"

"I do. I'm just starting to fade."

"Oh, no, you don't," Anthony said. "If you want to be my equal, you have to keep up with me."

"Oh, no," she groaned. "I hate men who get a second wind."

"Shut up and stay awake," he said, parroting a variation on her earlier instructions to him.

"Where are you going?" she asked as he got out of bed.

"I bought a little something to get your attention," he said, heading off to the kitchen.

In the kitchen he opened the freezer, got out the giant bag of M&M's and headed back to Nicole with a smile on his face.

A very, very wicked smile.

Entering the bedroom, he approached Nicole, opening the bag on the way to the bed.

She giggled as he shook the bag to tempt her. "You are a bad man, Anthony Gawain."

"And you love it, Ms. Hart."

"Ohh . . . Anthony, that's cold!"

"It'll melt, I promise."

"Anthony!"

"Umm."

THE CLOCK RADIO CAME on, waking her rudely with the boisterous laugh of the latest shock jock to rule the airwaves.

Nicole hit the snooze button out of force of habit.

She had been only partially honest with Anthony. It was true that she was grouchy when she woke up. But she was grouchy whether she got her way or not.

Still, in the twilight zone of awakening, she lay in bed, letting the events of the long afternoon and night play in her mind like some hazy sentimental commercial—a very naughty one.

As she slowly came awake, cold reality surfaced to hit her in the face.

No matter how much she wanted to, she couldn't put off telling Anthony the truth this morning. She had to confess that she was a waitress and an aspiring screenwriter—both a far cry from the sex therapist she'd been pretending to be.

She stretched her arms over her head and stiffened her legs to loosen the kinks of a night's sleep—a short night's sleep. Anthony's dark hair, spread on her white pillow, was an erotic image that would forever be imprinted on her mind. That, and the the way passion darkened his sexy green eyes when they made love.

She turned to look at him.

He wasn't there.

The bed was empty.

She felt the space where he'd slept. It was still warm.

He must have gotten up and gone to the kitchen for coffee, she surmised. In fact, now that she listened carefully, she could hear the television in the living room. She smiled as she recognized the familiar *beep, beep* of her favorite cartoon. Anthony Gawain was a man of "cultured" tastes.

And he was a dear for letting her sleep.

Throwing back the quilt, she got out of bed and groaned when she caught a glimpse of herself in the mirror.

She needed a major miracle.

She walked closer to the mirror, braving the daylight. Up close it wasn't so bad. She had this silly glow. Despite the lack of makeup and any discernible hairstyle, she looked sort of okay.

Maybe it was the way Anthony made her feel about herself.

Good. He made her feel good about herself.

He'd seen her at her worst, and he hadn't run out on her, which was what she would have expected from a handsome, charismatic man like him. He'd stayed and made her feel special.

Anthony Gawain was an amazing man.

She pulled the quilt over the sheets, making up the bed, and fluffed the pillows against the white-and-gold iron scrollwork headboard.

A smile lifted the corners of her mouth when she saw the open bag of M&M's on the nightstand. Popping one in her mouth, she turned the radio to a music station as it came back on. Elton John was belting out "You're the One." Nicole was humming along in agreement when she went to take her shower.

Going down the hall, she inhaled the scent of fresh coffee brewing in the kitchen.

He was an amazing man.

He seemed to have taken her "What women really want is a wife" comment to heart. Well, it was the truth. It was what most women she knew wanted. They needed someone to nurture them.

Someone to tuck in their blankets and make them toast and juice when they were sick. Instead of being strong and silent and afraid of losing them.

Someone to kiss them and make it better. Instead of ranting about how unfair his boss was.

Someone to put salt and a shovel in the trunk of the car. Instead of saying women couldn't drive in snow.

Someone to send them a card for no reason. Instead of on special occasions only.

Someone to just hold them—and nothing more—when they needed a hug.

She smiled.

Someone who remembered you liked plain and not peanut.

After taking her shower, Nicole looked through her closet, trying to make up her mind about what to wear for her confession. She needed Rafe's opinion.

Finally she settled on an ivory linen sleeveless shirt and a pair of khaki linen walking shorts. After gelling her hair, putting in pearl ear studs and applying brown-black mascara and a slash of scarlet lipstick, she went out to own up to her lie.

If she didn't tell him now, she'd lose her nerve.

Taking a deep breath, she went to the kitchen for coffee and confession.

The room was empty.

Sunny and bright, with a pot of fresh coffee perking, but empty. Puzzled, she walked over to the rattan table by the double window, which was half-curtained with white eyelet. A single tangerine rose, looking suspiciously like one from her neighbor's prize rosebush, stood in a glass vase in the center of the table.

Anthony's half-filled mug of coffee sat beside the L.A. *Times* he'd brought in. Bemusedly she wondered if anyone ever got up early enough to see it delivered. More likely it would be someone coming home late enough.

She decided he must have gone to the bathroom. There weren't many places to be in such a small house.

Pouring a cup of coffee to steady her nerves, she peered into the refrigerator to see if anything interesting had magically appeared since she'd last looked.

Besides her three staples of old cheese, limp celery and pickles were eggs, butter and a loaf of bread.

She took out the bread and butter to make toast. She could think better on a full stomach, she reasoned. When the toast popped up, she buttered it, then went in search of Anthony, licking butter from her fingers.

The bathroom was empty.

He wasn't in the bedroom when she rechecked it, or the living room, or the hall.

It wasn't a good sign.

Had Anthony just run off?

No, she was being ridiculous. Paranoid.

He was probably outside getting something out of his Jeep. A pencil, maybe, to work the crossword puzzle. Men liked to do that sort of thing.

Or...maybe he was making a call on his car phone. A call he didn't want her to overhear, paranoia suggested.

She looked outside, and her heart fell.

Opening the door, she ventured outside to make sure, and confirmed her worst suspicion.

His Jeep was gone, and so was he.

She'd been stupid, stupid, stupid....

Anthony Gawain was a creep.

She went back inside to see if the cad had had the decency to leave a note. Unreasonably hoping there might be a logical reason why he had left. Instead of the "same old," he was a handsome charismatic charmer. Instead of the "same old," she was a foolish woman. What was she thinking that she could hold such a man for more than just a night? Much less a book.

And then it hit her that he still didn't know the truth about her. And, spitefully, she was glad.

It served him right.

Returning to the kitchen to get her cup of coffee, she slumped down in one of the rattan chairs at the table.

It was then that she saw it.

The newspaper was open at the Entertainment News column. She scanned it quickly and saw with a sinking feeling in the pit of her stomach just why Anthony had left. And she didn't blame him.

*Los Angeles Times*

Entertainment News:

ITEM . . . As you all know, my darlings, nothing in Hollywood is what it appears. Hollywood is the land of makebelieve. Along that line, my sources have discovered that Nicole Hart is not a sex therapist at all, but a writer. This columnist wonders if Anthony Gawain was in on the scam, or if he's been scammed. Wouldn't that be delicious? Rumor has it that the two have been tapped by a prestigious publisher to coauthor a book based on the ratings of their successful pairing on the What Do Women Want? segment Nicole Hart appeared on during sweeps week. Do tell us, is it true? Or…could it be, the sly Ms. Hart is penning a tell-all book about the powerful Gawain political dynasty?

Anthony Gawain probably thought the worst of her.

And she could hardly blame him. Why hadn't she told him the truth last night?

She had to find him and confess.

She held her head in her hands and tried to decide what to do. How to rectify the biggest screwup of her life—so far.

Where would Anthony go? Where could she find him?

She remembered he had a taping for his anniversary show. His show had been running for a year, and the network was after him to renew his contract.

Hadn't he mentioned something last night about being ready for a change?

The phone rang, interrupting her thoughts, and she picked it up.

"Nicole, I've been waiting for you to call me. What's going on with Mother?"

Oh, drat! She'd forgotten to call her sister back.

"Ah, Wendy... Can I call you back?"

"Why? What's going— Nicole, do you have a man there?"

"I'll call you back," she said, hanging up.

The phone rang again.

"Wendy, I said—"

"It's not Wendy, it's Peter," Rafe said, deadpan. "Listen, Dorothy, has Toto brought the morning paper in yet? Lady, you're in a mess of trouble."

"Oh, Rafe, what am I going to do?"

# 12

"THE PRESS ISN'T welcome here, Nikki. So why don't you just leave?" Anthony said when he opened the door of his Malibu home to find her on his doorstep with a picnic basket in hand. "Is there a tape recorder hidden in there?"

He was The Ice Man, devoid of feeling.

"I'm not leaving," she declared, setting down the basket.

"I don't have anything to say to you, Nikki. I don't give interviews—at least not when I know I'm being interviewed, anyway."

"You have to let me explain," she insisted.

"There's nothing for you to explain. I can read, like everyone else. You scammed me. All that show of angry hurt over my not telling you about coauthoring— You're good, really good. If you decide to change careers, you should go into acting. I'll give you a rave review." His green eyes raked her. "You got what you wanted, Nikki, so just . . . just go."

"But it wasn't like that, Anthony."

"Indeed?" He arched a dark brow. "Are you trying to tell me you *are* a sex therapist?"

"No."

"Are you telling me you aren't a writer?"

"No."

"I rest my case. Goodbye."

He closed the door. Firmly.

She rang the doorbell again.

He didn't answer.

After several more tries, she decided he wasn't going to answer the doorbell's peals. She sat down on the front steps. Inside, she could hear him playing some sort of opera at full volume on his sound system.

If he thought the music was going to drive her away, he was wrong. It was the perfect background for high drama. It actually inspired her to remain stubborn.

He owed her an opportunity to explain.

She'd given *him* one.

Opening the picnic basket, she took out a box of Oreo cookies and a bottle of wine. Uncorking the bottle, she began drinking from it and eating the cookies.

After about an hour the music stopped.

The Oreo cookies were almost gone, but the bottle of wine was still nearly full. She'd reached the point of action. She wasn't going down without a fight.

Uncorking the bottle of wine, she poured the contents into the bushes. Then she laid it on its side so that Anthony would see that it was empty and jump to the conclusion she wanted—that she was very tipsy.

Stone-cold sober, she rang the doorbell.

After a few minutes, the door opened. "I told you to go away."

"Ah, Anthony..." she began. "Stand still..." she said, blinking and weaving. He thought she was a great actress, so she'd give him a great performance. Whatever it took to get his attention—to get him to listen to her.

"I...ah...think I'm going to be—" She lurched forward into the foyer.

He caught her. "For Pete's sake, Nikki, you smell like a winery," he complained, trying to get her to stand on her own two feet to no avail. It was like trying to stand a piece of cooked spaghetti on its end. She let her body go limp and flailed her arms around his neck. "That and a chocolate factory," he muttered.

"That's 'cause I had a little wine-and-cookie party...." She giggled, carrying on the pretense of being tipsy.

"Anthony—?"

"What?"

"I don't feel so good right now."

Swinging her up into his arms with a resigned sigh, he carried her to the powder room and set her down, holding her head over the porcelain bowl.

"Anthony..."

"What is it?"

"I'm not really a sex therapist, did you know that?"

"I believe I read that somewhere recently," he answered coldly.

She nodded, hitting her head on the porcelain. "Ouch!" She rubbed her head, thinking perhaps she was getting into character a little too much.

Anthony groaned.

"I'm not," she continued. "I know I said I was, but I'm not."

"Keep your head down. You'll feel better," he said when she tried to turn to talk to him.

"Anthony..."

"What?"

"I should have told you I tell stories...."

"You should have told me," he agreed, his voice clipped.

"No. Wait, that's not right. I mean write. I write stories," she said, keeping up the pretense with her disjointed speech.

"One assumes. You won't mind if I don't give a damn. As long as I'm not in them, that is."

"I write stories about people. Pay attention," she said, not having to feign exasperation. "But I don't write about real people."

"What do you mean, you don't write about real people?" he demanded, turning to look at her as he dampened the washcloth beneath the faucet.

"What I'm trying to tell you, if you'll just stop judging me for a moment and listen, is that I make up stories for the movies."

"You mean you're a screenwriter?" he demanded, incredulous.

"Yes. That's what I've been trying to tell you."

"For heaven's sake, why didn't you tell me that, Nikki? Do you know what I was thinking? I thought you were..." He leaned forward with the damp washcloth in his hand.

"Were you planning to give me another bath?" she asked, all trace of being tipsy dropping from her voice and demeanor.

"Why, you're sober, aren't you? You aren't the least bit—" he said, realizing the truth.

"That's right. I only pretended to be tipsy so I could get inside and talk to you. I even let you lead me into the bathroom and shove my head in the toilet, just so I—" She started to cry, beginning to feel really foolish crouched beside the porcelain bowl.

"Don't cry," he said, pulling her up and setting her on the sink as she continued sobbing.

"Please..." he begged, wiping at her tears, then handing her the damp washcloth. "Why are you crying?"

"I'm...I'm crying because I'm tired of playing games, of pretending." She sniffed. "Because I thought I'd lost you. I thought I'd lost you because you believed I was lying to you. And it would have been ironic, because I was lying to you because I thought I'd lose you if I told you the truth."

"Maybe you are tipsy. You're not making any sense," he said, furrowing his brow. "I don't understand what the hell you were just saying."

Nicole folded the washcloth in her hands and looked down at it. "Don't you see? We've both been lying to each other, because we were afraid to be vulnerable—afraid to risk being hurt. We've been stupid, letting our pride cheat us out of a chance at happiness.

"All I ever wanted, Anthony—all any woman really wants—is someone to love her enough to be honest with her. Love can't grow in a patch of half-truths. Lies are like weeds, they'll grow until they eventually choke out any chance for love to thrive.

"Every woman is different. What she wants—what I want—is a man to discover and care for who they are . . . even if they're sometimes difficult and foolish and—"

He pulled her into his arms. "Impossibly sexy," he finished for her. "Do you think we could start over, Nikki?"

"I'd like that. There's only one thing better in a story than a happy ending . . ." she said, kissing the corner of his lips.

"What's that?" he asked, returning her caress.

"The *good part*," she answered, slipping away to turn on the shower.

A half hour later, when they were out of the hot water and well on their way to starting over with nothing between them but the truth, Anthony reached for a dry towel with a chuckle.

"What?" Nicole asked, taking the towel from him.

"I always wondered what good clean sex was...."

He jumped out of the way as she snapped the towel at him.

*Los Angeles Times*

Entertainment News: ITEM ... *What Do Women Want?* Evidently it's Anthony Gawain and Nicole Hart's hot new book of the same title. It hit the New York *Times* list, debuting at number ten, and hasn't looked back on its way to the number-one spot. My sources tell me Hollywood is also interested in Ms. Hart's romantic comedy, *Cat and Spouse.* Seems they want Anthony and Nicole to play the principal parts in the screenplay. The duo is going to be autographing books today at The Book Emporium in Long Beach. This columnist wishes them every success. Can a *What Do Men Want?* sequel be in the works? Stay tuned.

"Can you believe it?" Nicole asked, handing the column over to Anthony. "We're really number one on the New York *Times* list! And did you see that about the screenplay? Our agent is working overtime."

"Yes, he's been almost as giddy as I have since he's taken you on," Anthony answered, resigned to being bedazzled by his coauthor. "And to think the book almost didn't happen. That we almost didn't forgive each other for being so stubborn."

"Well, it was all your fault. You were the stubborn one," she said, putting on a pair of outrageous Lunch At The Ritz earrings her mother had bought at Nancy's Gallery in Kimmswick, Missouri, when she'd been in St. Louis for a rodeo last week. The earrings were fanciful, with tiny boots and spurs and other assorted cowboy gear dangling from them.

"*I* was stubborn?" Anthony repeated.

"Yes, you were the one who wouldn't let me explain that I had wanted to tell you I wasn't a sex therapist, but I was afraid, knowing your passion for the truth, that you wouldn't forgive me for my harmless charade."

"Harmless? Do you know how fancy our agent had to talk to convince the publisher that it didn't matter that you weren't a sex therapist? That it wasn't important to the book. That an everyman's guide was better than all the books with experts' pat solutions. He only convinced them after showing them the tape of the show we did together."

"Yeah, I know. But you were hardly harmless, either. You wanted a sex therapist to help you write the book, but instead of saying it was a business proposition, you romanced me."

"I didn't plan that. That just happened."

Finished putting in her earrings, Nicole buzzed his ear with a kiss. "I'm glad it did," she whispered.

There was a knock on the door, and Anthony went to answer it.

"The publisher sent a limo. The driver is waiting."

"A limo? They really sent a limo?" she said excitedly, grabbing her purse.

"Don't go getting any ideas," he warned as they left to go to the autographing.

She behaved herself during the limo ride. Anthony swore it was only because she was wearing a white linen suit that would wrinkle. He liked how she wore only a matching white linen vest under it, without a blouse. The flowers he'd arranged to have sent to the store would be perfect with it.

There was a crowd waiting when they arrived. Nicole was surprised to see how many faces she recognized when she got inside.

"Mother!" she cried, when her two sisters walked up with her in tow. "You'll never guess what Mother has been up to," Wendy said. Her other sister, Suzanne, mouthed the words, "Don't ask."

But she couldn't help herself. "You got married, didn't you? Where is he?" Nicole asked, looking around.

"No, she didn't get married. I wish she had," Wendy replied.

"What? What did you do now, Mother?"

"I bought a horse."

"A horse!"

Her mother nodded with excitement while her sisters rolled their eyes.

"Mother, what are you going to do with a horse?" Nicole asked.

"Why, race him, of course."

"But you don't know anything about racing horses," Nicole objected.

"That's what we told her," her sisters chorused.

"That's what I've got a trainer for," their mother explained, smiling wickedly.

*"Mo-ther!"*

She turned to Anthony. "Tell me, Mr. Gawain, how did I manage to raise three stick-in-the-muds like these."

*"Mo-ther!"*

Anthony laughed. "I don't know ma'am. But I have to tell you, there are times when Nikki does you proud."

"Really?"

Her mother and sisters turned to look at her.

"We have books to sign, Anthony," Nicole reminded, tugging him over to the table and the pretty woman who had set up the autographing.

"Hey, lady, will you sign one for me? I want it autographed, 'To the last of the great lovers . . .'"

"Rafe! What are you doing here?" Nicole asked, taking the book he wanted her to autograph, helplessly watching her mother and sisters pumping Anthony for information.

"Elizabeth said I have to buy it—and read it."

Nicole laughed and signed it exactly as he'd asked.

"Where is Elizabeth?" she questioned.

"I lost her on the way over here. I think she's out sizing solitaires."

"Rafe!"

"I know. What is it with you women and wedding brain?" he asked as Anthony joined them to sign books for the line that was forming.

At the end of three hours, the autographing was over, and everyone had gone on ahead to meet them at Sofi's Patio Restaurant for a celebration party.

Just then, a deliveryman appeared, holding up a florist's box. "These are for Ms. Nicole Hart," he said.

"Thanks," Anthony said, tipping him.

"What are these for?" Nicole asked, taking a bouquet of white tulips from the long white box. "Are they from you?"

"Read the card," he said, pointing it out.

Nicole slipped her pink manicured nail beneath the flap and withdrew the tiny card. When she read it, she squealed with delight.

"Is that a yes or a no, or did you see a mouse in the box?" Anthony asked, deadpan.

"It's a yes, you idiot!"

"Idiot? How can you call your groom an idiot?"

"'Cause you were foolish enough to ask me in black-and-white!" she flipped back, waving the florist's card, with his scrawled "Will you marry me? Love

Anthony," high in the air. "I'll sue you for alienation of affection if you get cold feet. I swear I will."

"I don't have time to get cold feet," he said, smiling.

"What do you mean?"

"I mean everyone, including the minister, and Rafe, with your custom-designed veil, is waiting at Sofi's for the wedding."

"What?"

He nodded.

"You mean my mother and sisters, Rafe, your family..."

He nodded. "Even Mark."

"But what if I'd said no?" she asked, laughing uproariously at his stunt. His damned fine romantic stunt.

"Read the back of the card."

She turned it over. The tiny print read: "If the answer is no, I'll be at the bridge. Briefly."

She threw her arms around him.

"You're an amazing man, Anthony Gawain."

"I'll take that in black-and-white, too," he said, handing her one of their books to autograph.

And so they were married in a black-and-white wedding.

The wedding album would show a blushing bride, a grinning groom, a mother catching the bridal bouquet, and a costume designer catching the garter.

And a white limo pulling away with a Just Married sign on the back, and no visible sign of the bride and groom inside.

"SO, RAFE, DID YOU finish reading Anthony and Nicole's book?"

"Yes, Elizabeth."

"What was the conclusion?"

"Conclusion?"

"Yeah, you know. What do women want?"

"Honesty."

"Hmm . . . Do you like what I'm wearing?"

"Ah . . ."

"Rafe . . ."

"It's not my favorite outfit of yours, okay?"

"What is your favorite?"

"Your birthday suit," he answered, lowering the zipper of her long black dress to reveal that she'd recently been on a shopping spree at a Victoria's Secret store.

"Now, this is very nice," he said, snapping a black satin garter.

"I didn't spend a bloody fortune for *nice!*" Elizabeth said. "*Nice,*" she fumed. "*Nice* is a four-letter word."

Rafe's brown eyes gleamed with devilish desire. "In that case, may I suggest a better one?"

# Epilogue

ANTHONY AND NICOLE sat in the living room of their Malibu home, watching their four-year-old son, Anthony, pretend he was a carpenter. He had on a play tool belt and was hammering away.

"You're supposed to be reading my script," Nicole said.

"And you're supposed to be rewriting it," he countered.

Both beamed at the light of their lives. "Is he really that adorable, or is it just because he's ours?" Nicole asked.

"Probably the latter," Anthony said.

And then they both shook their head in unison. "Naw..."

"Do you think he's going to like Paris?" Nicole asked, watching their small son pretend to measure something. The screenplay she'd just sold was called *French Kiss*, and it was set in Paris. It was the third in the film series that had started with their successful pairing in *Cat and Spouse*.

They had never written the sequel *What Do Men Want?*—the standing joke between them being, Who would buy a book with just one word in it?

"Have you seen the sketches Rafe sent over for our costumes?" she asked.

"Do I have to wear a beret?" he asked, lifting a dark eyebrow.

"I could arrange it," she told him teasingly. "I think you'd look quite dashing in one, with your ponytail."

"I should never leave you and Rafe alone together," he groaned. "I know. I'll keep him busy doing some props for my special on royalty." Anthony had given up his weekly talk show soon after they'd married in favor of doing the occasional special in between the movies they made together.

He squatted down to his son's level and asked him what he was doing.

His son told him he was wallpapering. Anthony and Nicole had added a level onto the house, and the little boy was fascinated by all the workmen, mimicking their jobs.

"So, Anthony," he said, ruffling his son's hair, "have you decided what you're going to be when you grow up?"

"I'm going to be in 'struction," he told his father proudly.

"What are you going to do in 'struction?"

"I'm going to paper and build and put in pipes."

Anthony laughed. "Son, you're going to have to choose just one of those jobs and do it really well."

"Oh."

"What do you think you'll be, then?" Nicole asked from the sofa.

Her son thought for a moment and then answered. "I'm going to be in the job with the best tools."

Their eyes met over their son's head, smiling, as he went about his play.

Nicole rose from the carpet, crooking her finger at her husband.

"What?" he asked, standing and pulling her into his arms.

"I have this job in mind...." she said sexily.

"Really, Mrs. Gawain?"

She nodded. "I was wondering if you could help me out. You see, I require a workman who has the best..."

"*Really, Mrs. Gawain!*"

"You can call me Nikki."

Anthony swung her up into his arms to carry her upstairs as the nanny came back from her shopping trip.

When they reached the master-bedroom door, she just happened to mention that her mother was coming to celebrate Anthony's birthday that weekend.

Melting him with a kiss, she added, "And she's bringing him a very special present."

"Really? What?"

"Don't ask."

Much, much later, he had the presence of mind to ask, "Sweetheart, what are we going to do with a pony?"

## A Note from Tiffany White

I spent my childhood in a number of orphanages and foster homes. Books were my escape, and fairy tales figured prominently in my emotional survival. They taught me values, the magic in believing and that there is always a handsome prince. So what if he's the one who sometimes needs rescuing.

For the Lovers & Legends miniseries I wanted to write about the legend of Sir Gawain's marriage because of its contemporary message. When Sir Anthony went in search of the answer to the question *Which thing is it which women most desire?*, he could find no definitive answer. The reason is that each woman is an individual—unique and special. Every woman has her own wants, her own desires.

A man of honor, a hero like Sir Gawain, brings forth a woman's true beauty with his trust, his love and his acceptance. And so it is with my my 1990's version of Anthony Gawain.

I suppose fairy tales were the beginning of my love affair with the romance genre. I hope Nicole Hart and Anthony Gawain enchant you in *Naughty Talk,* thereby allowing me to return the pleasure of all the fairy tales I have read and continue to enjoy.

Relive the romance...
Harlequin and Silhouette
are proud to present

A program of collections of three complete novels by the most-requested
authors with the most-requested themes. Be sure to look for one volume each
month with three complete novels by top-name authors.

In September: **BAD BOYS**     Dixie Browning
              Ann Major
              Ginna Gray
*No heart is safe when these hot-blooded hunks are in town!*

In October:  **DREAMSCAPE**   Jayne Ann Krentz
              Anne Stuart
              Bobby Hutchinson
*Something's happening! But is it love or magic?*

In December: **SOLUTION: MARRIAGE** Debbie Macomber
                  Annette Broadrick
                  Heather Graham Pozzessere
*Marriages in name only have a way of leading to love....*

**Available at your favorite retail outlet.**

REQ-G2

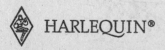 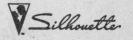

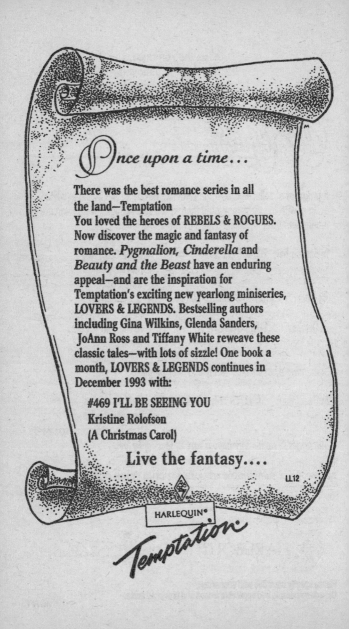

## Once upon a time...

There was the best romance series in all the land—Temptation You loved the heroes of REBELS & ROGUES. Now discover the magic and fantasy of romance. *Pygmalion, Cinderella* and *Beauty and the Beast* have an enduring appeal—and are the inspiration for Temptation's exciting new yearlong miniseries, LOVERS & LEGENDS. Bestselling authors including Gina Wilkins, Glenda Sanders, JoAnn Ross and Tiffany White reweave these classic tales—with lots of sizzle! One book a month, LOVERS & LEGENDS continues in December 1993 with:

#469 I'LL BE SEEING YOU
Kristine Rolofson
(A Christmas Carol)

### Live the fantasy....

LL12

HARLEQUIN®

*Temptation*

HARLEQUIN®

*Temptation*

## FIRST-PERSON PERSONAL

Nothing is more intimate than first-person personal narration....

Two emotionally intense, intimate romances told in first person, in the tradition of Daphne du Maurier's *Rebecca* from bestselling author Janice Kaiser.

Recently widowed Allison Stephens travels to her husband's home to discover the truth about his death and finds herself caught up in a web of family secrets and betrayals. Even more dangerous is the passion ignited in her by the man her husband hated most—Dirk Granville.
BETRAYAL, Temptation #462, October 1993

P.I. Darcy Hunter is drawn into the life of Kyle Weston, the man who had been engaged to her deceased sister. Seeing him again sparks long-buried feelings of love and guilt. Working closely together on a case, their attraction escalates. But Darcy fears it is memories of her sister that Kyle is falling in love with.
DECEPTIONS, Temptation #466, November 1993

Each book tells you the heroine's compelling story in her own personal voice. Wherever Harlequin books are sold.

If you missed *Betrayal* (TE #462), order your copy now by sending your name, address, zip or postal code along with a check or money order (please do not send cash) for $2.99, plus 75¢ postage and handling ($1.00 in Canada), payable to Harlequin Books, to:

| In the U.S. | In Canada |
|---|---|
| 3010 Walden Avenue | P.O. Box 609 |
| P.O. Box 1325 | Fort Erie, Ontario |
| Buffalo, NY 14269-1325 | L2A 5X3 |

Please specify book title with your order.
Canadian residents add applicable federal and provincial taxes.

HTFPP1

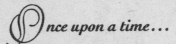

*Once upon a time...*

## THERE WAS A FABULOUS
## PROOF-OF-PURCHASE OFFER
## AVAILABLE FROM

As you enjoy your Harlequin Temptation LOVERS & LEGENDS stories each and every month during 1993, you can collect four proofs of purchase to redeem a lovely opal pendant! The classic look of opals is always in style, and this necklace is a perfect complement to any outfit!

One proof of purchase can be found in the back pages of each LOVERS & LEGENDS title...one every month during 1993!

### LIVE THE FANTASY...

To receive your gift, mail this certificate, along with four (4) proof-of-purchase coupons from any Harlequin Temptation LOVERS & LEGENDS title plus $2.50 for postage and handling (check or money order—do not send cash), payable to Harlequin Books, to: **In the U.S.:** LOVERS & LEGENDS, P.O. Box 9069, Buffalo, NY 14269-9069; **In Canada:** LOVERS & LEGENDS, P.O. Box 626, Fort Erie, Ontario L2A 5X3.
Requests must be received by January 31, 1994.
Allow 4-6 weeks after receipt of order for delivery.

NAME: _____

ADDRESS: _____

_____

CITY: _____

STATE/PROVINCE: _____

ZIP/POSTAL CODE: _____

ACCOUNT NO.: _____

ONE PROOF OF PURCHASE                083 KAO LLPOPDIRR